Into the

Valley

Into the Valley

THE SETTLERS

Rosanne Bittner

A Tom Doherty Associates Book
New York

This is a work of fiction. All the characters and events portrayed in this novel are either fictitious or are used fictitiously.

INTO THE VALLEY: THE SETTLERS

This book is printed on acid-free paper.

A Forge Book
Published by Tom Doherty Associates, LLC.
175 Fifth Avenue
New York, NY 10010

www.tor.com

Forge® is a registered trademark of Tom Doherty Associates, LLC.

Library of Congress Cataloging-in-Publication Data

Bittner, Rosanne, 1945–
    Into the valley : the settlers / Rosanne Bittner.—1st ed.
        p. cm.
    "A Tom Doherty Associates book."
    ISBN: 0-765-30065-6 (alk. paper)
    1. Ohio River Valley—History—Revolution, 1775–1783—Fiction. 2. Triangles (Interpersonal relations)—Fiction. 3. Frontier and pioneer life—Fiction. 4. Women pioneers—Fiction. 5. Brothers—Fiction. I. Title.

PS3552.I77396 I56 2003
813'.54—dc21

2002035383

First Edition: March 2003

Printed in the United States of America

0 9 8 7 6 5 4 3 2 1

To the brave souls who have fought for the freedom America enjoys, from the first revolutionaries to those who now fight terrorism

AUTHOR'S NOTE

This "America West" series would be impossible to write without the vast historical resources I have found in books by Allan W. Eckert such as *The Frontiersmen, That Dark and Bloody River, The Conquerors*, and *Wilderness Empire* (Little, Brown & Co., Toronto, Canada). Also, for this particular story, *The Revolutionary War* by Bart McDowell (National Geographic Society) was a great help. I urge anyone who loves reading about America's history, or who teaches the subject, to read these books.

When writing about America's history, I prefer to include some of the lesser-known people and battles rather than focus on the famous events we learn about in school. We have to remember that it wasn't just the famous characters we read about who won freedom for this country. They could not have done it without the thousands upon thousands of brave colonists who risked everything they owned, as well as their very lives, to create these United States of America. Most of their names will never appear in history books.

This book and all others I write are full of real historical events and locations; however, the main characters are fictitious. The settlement called Willow Creek in this story, although much like real frontier settlements of the time, is also fictitious. And although this is my fictitious story, I have no doubt that the events portrayed in these pages run parallel with real-life stories from the past.

In this tale, I mention Noah and Jess Wilde. Their personal story is told in my book *Into the Wilderness,* the first book of my "America West" series.

Into the Valley

I

July 10, 1780
Willow Creek, Ohio Valley

Annie set out a blackberry pie she'd baked herself, then stepped back to view the grand display of food brought in by the women of Willow Creek. It was all laid out on a long table made of boards set on top of barrels, then covered with tablecloths.

Aside from her upcoming marriage, Annie was sure this day would become one of her best memories. Most of the population of Willow Creek was here to help build Luke Wilde's barn, one of the finishing touches to the biggest farm in the area—a farm she would soon share with Luke.

"Annie Barnes, I'm so jealous!"

Annie turned to share a smile with her good friend, Jenny Carlson. "Of what?" she teased.

"You know what! You snagged the most handsome, most successful man in the Ohio Valley!"

Annie laughed. "I don't know if you'd call it snagging. You know good and well that Luke and I have been friends since we were kids. He and his brother are practically part of the family. It's not like Luke and I suddenly met and I had to run after him." She looked back at the barn, watching Luke, so handsome and strong. He was helping another man place a handhewn support beam. "Luke told me he's known he wanted to marry me since I was twelve years old."

Jenny grabbed her hand and squeezed it. "Everybody knew you and Luke would end up together," she told Annie. "My brothers used to make bets on it. Sam said Luke would marry you, and Clete said it would be Jeremiah."

Annie felt a tiny pain in her chest at the mention of Luke's brother. "Oh?" She looked back at Jenny, forcing herself to keep a smile on her face. "Why on earth would I marry a wandering man like Jeremiah?"

Jenny laughed. "Because he was crazy about you once himself, you know. And Lord knows, it's a hard decision as to which brother is the best looking. That Jeremiah, he used to make my heart pound back before he left three years ago, and I was only thirteen then, not even old enough to be thinking that way about a man. Did you know that Jeremiah and Luke had a big fight over you right before Jeremiah left?"

Now it became a struggle for Annie to keep smiling and appear unaffected. "No! Are you serious?"

"You *didn't* know, did you? My brothers ordered me to keep it a secret, but now that you're marrying Luke—"

Annie's mother began clanging a cowbell, interrupting the conversation. "Time to eat!" she hollered at the men working on the barn. Several of the men let out whoops and whistles, clamoring down from the still-open rafters to wash hands and faces at water barrels.

"I'm going to find Larry!" Jenny told Annie. "He promised to eat with me!"

Annie watched her friend run off to find Larry Klug, a young man from distant Fort Harmar who'd lately been calling on Jenny as often as possible while the summer weather allowed it. Jenny's wildly curly, dark hair fluttered every which way as she ran, and Annie lost sight of her as men began gathering around the table of food. Preacher Patrick Falls, who'd come to Willow Creek two years ago to minister to the settlers, called out that they should all pray before eating.

Now Luke was beside Annie, moving a hand to her waist. She glanced up at him before prayer, thinking how he looked even more handsome when he was tanned and sweating from the hot sun. His thick, dark hair fell recklessly about his face, its color and the tan only accenting his amazingly blue eyes. Luke smiled down at her proudly. Annie knew he was bursting with joy at finally getting the barn finished before they would marry. The wedding was set for less than two weeks from now.

Preacher Falls prayed, but Annie didn't hear the words. Jeremiah and Luke had fought over her? Did Jeremiah tell Luke what happened—that night in the barn—between her and himself? Surely not! Luke would never have asked her to marry him if he knew.

Why? Why had she allowed that to happen? It never should have; but it was Jeremiah she'd loved dearly. It was Jeremiah she'd had that terrible crush on, in spite of Luke being the one who gave her all the attention. Jeremiah—always the wanderer—gone more than he was home, the one who loved to hunt and who even spent time on occasion with a friendly band of Delaware Indians. It was Jeremiah who dressed in buckskins and wore his near-black hair long like those wild Indians—Jeremiah whose skin was even darker than Luke's, and who had eyes black as coal.

Back then, people called Jeremiah the "wild one." Luke was the brother who had stayed put and worked hard. Luke had built this wonderful farm, and had even built a fine stone house for his betrothed. Soon she would live in that sturdy, beautiful home with Luke. There she would bear and raise his children, the wife of the most eligible man in the Ohio Valley. Luke was the brother who had pursued her and asked her to marry him, and there was not one thing about him for a woman not to love.

She did indeed love him, but she'd also loved his brother. And it was his brother who had seduced her that night in the barn at her parents' farm . . . his brother who had a way of casting a spell on her and making her do foolish things . . . his brother who had taken her first.

While the preacher prayed his thanks for the food they were about to eat, Annie prayed that Luke would never find out how passionately she'd loved Jeremiah, how foolish she'd been that night, how deeply hurt she'd been when Jeremiah left after that—three years ago—never to come back. Why had he done that after making love to her? Never had she felt so abandoned and heartbroken; yet she couldn't share her pain, because she also couldn't share the reason for it, the secret sin she'd committed.

She knew now how wrong it had been to give herself to a man like Jeremiah. Even if he'd stayed around and married her, their marriage would have been a disaster. Jeremiah was not the marrying type. He and Luke were as different as night and day. Luke was the stable farmer, a man who would always be around to protect and provide for his wife and family. Jeremiah, the wanderer, would have been gone much more than at home.

People were talking and visiting now, standing in line to eat. Luke, her wonderful Luke, was right behind her, talking and laughing, a man happy to be finishing his barn, happy to be getting married soon. Oh, how she loved him! If only she'd known life would turn out this way, she never would have shared that night with Jeremiah.

Now she felt angry with Jenny for bringing up the subject,

spoiling such a wonderful day. She smiled as she handed Luke
a plate so he could fill it with beans and ham and biscuits and
pie. She pointed out her own berry pie, and he took a slice, giving
her a wink and smiling with full lips and even, white teeth. "I'm
not only marrying the prettiest girl in these parts, but also the
best cook," he told her.

Annie blushed, hoping her nose wasn't getting too red from
the sun. She thought how fair her skin was compared to Luke's
tanned hands. Her skin wouldn't take color. It simply burned
and peeled and stayed white. Her red freckles matched her red
hair, and Luke always told her that her green eyes made him
think of green apples. She hated her freckles, but Luke loved
them. Her heart rushed at the thought of sharing his bed in only
two more weeks. She just hoped . . . could a man tell if a woman
wasn't a virgin? Maybe not when it was only once, and after all,
it had been three years ago. Much as she'd been crazy about
Jeremiah, she now loved Luke in a different, deeper way, and
she couldn't stand the thought of how hurt he'd be if he knew
what she'd done.

Now the air was full of talk and laughter and forks hitting
dishes. Younger children ran and played, ducking around those
who were eating, chasing dogs and chickens. Men teased Luke
about his upcoming marriage, and women talked about quilting
and recipes. Annie's brothers, seventeen-year-old Jake and fifteen-
year-old Calvin, sat on a log with Luke. They adored him, as did
her little sister, twelve-year-old Sally, who walked around pouring
coffee for the men.

Yes, this was a good day after all. She would soon be Mrs.
Luke Wilde. This was not a day for thinking about a mistake
she'd made three years ago. Women began filling their own
plates, but Annie couldn't eat. The excitement of the day, combined with the heat, brought little appetite . . . and Jenny's com-

ment about the fight between Luke and Jeremiah disturbed her. Luke had never mentioned it. Why not?

Before long, people began moaning about being too full. There was more visiting and laughter, and some of the men lay back in the grass to rest a bit before returning to work on the barn. In the distance, Luke's fields were ripening with corn and potatoes. Cattle grazed in another field, and chickens clucked and strutted everywhere. A few of Annie's mother's friends congratulated Annie and offered to help with the upcoming wedding.

"We're having Luke over tomorrow night to talk more about it," Ethel Barnes told her good friend, Hilda Pickens.

"And, of course, *I* will play the piano for the wedding," Hilda insisted.

"Of course you will! You're the only woman in Willow Creek who knows *how* to play the piano!" Ethel answered. The women all laughed, and Annie joined them. Neither she nor the others noticed at first that a rider was just then approaching the gathering. It was Annie who finally caught sight of him. He sat tall on his black horse, his long, dark hair blowing in the light, hot breeze, the fringes of his buckskin clothing dancing with the rhythm of his body as it moved to the horse's gait.

Annie's heart nearly stopped beating. It was Jeremiah! He'd come home!

2

J eremiah!"

The name was spoken by more than one person, all in surprise, some with joy, others with wariness. Everyone knew that Jeremiah Wilde had most likely run off to join in the revolutionary fighting taking place back East, a fight many here at Willow Creek, including Luke, disagreed with. People quieted and stared as Jeremiah halted his horse and dismounted. Luke walked toward him, and Annie could feel the tension between them.

One of Luke's neighbors, a big widowed man named John Hagan, stood up from where he'd been lying in the grass. "Well, if it ain't Jeremiah Wilde, come back to roost."

Jeremiah glanced at the man, and Annie watched him with a fiery mixture of emotions—love and hatred, joy and anger. For three years, no one knew if he was alive or dead. Wild he was, just like his name, and he surely looked as though that part of him had not changed.

"Not to roost," Jeremiah answered Hagan. "Just to visit."

"Long enough to get this whole settlement in trouble," Hagan answered. "You've been off fightin' on the side of the Patriots, ain't you? You comin' here will make them think we're *all* Patriots! You know what that could mean!"

"Mind your own business, John," Luke barked, still watching Jeremiah. "I haven't seen my brother in three years. He's got a right to come visit me and others here."

"I been helpin' on that barn all mornin'," Hagan grumbled. "Don't be tellin' me to mind my own business."

Luke shot the man a scowl. "I appreciate the help, John, but this is a family matter." He looked around at the other men. "I'd be glad if all of you went on back to work. I'm obliged to every one of you and can't thank you enough."

"Sure, Luke." The words came from Tom Pickens, a good, Christian man who was not one to quickly judge. "Come on, boys, let's get back to work and let Luke visit with his brother."

Annie watched with a pounding heart as the men ambled back to the barn. Several nodded to Jeremiah, some walked up and shook his hand, welcoming him home, and others ignored him, obviously not sure of what to think of him being here, a Patriot, visiting them during these dangerous times.

Annie felt a note of relief when Luke put out his hand and Jeremiah grasped it. The handshake grew into a quick embrace, each man slapping the other on the back. Whatever they had fought about when Jeremiah left, apparently it was all forgiven . . . or was it? Jeremiah glanced at the barn, turned and looked the farm over, studying the stone house, the crops, the cattle. His gaze continued around to the women . . . and to Annie. His dark eyes showed old feelings and Annie felt her cheeks flushing. Why? Why had he come back now? He couldn't have picked a worse time! She swallowed and nodded. "Hello, Jeremiah."

Jeremiah nodded. "Hello, Annie."

What was he thinking? How was he feeling?

"Jeremiah, come and have something to eat!" Annie's mother

called out to him. "It's good to see you again, and we're so glad you're all right, son. Come sit down here at the table." She pointed to a large stump of a log that had been rolled to the table and set on end like a chair. Annie's youngest brother, Calvin, hurried over to shake Jeremiah's hand and offered to take care of his horse. "Glad you're back, Jeremiah! I bet you hardly recognize me. I was only twelve when you left."

Jeremiah smiled. "Calvin?"

"Yes, sir!"

Jeremiah put a hand on the young man's shoulder. "Well, you sure did grow up!" By then, seventeen-year-old Jake was also greeting Jeremiah, and Jeremiah exclaimed at the "man" he'd become. He walked closer, and Annie wanted to crawl under the table. There was so much left unspoken between them. Did he still love her? Had he *ever* loved her? Surely he hadn't come back for her. Maybe after lying in the hay with him, he'd decided she was no better than a whore and that was why he left. And again she had to wonder just how much Luke knew.

"Hi, Jeremiah!" Annie's younger sister ran up and hugged the man. "Remember me?"

Jeremiah frowned teasingly, holding her at arm's length. "You can't be Sally!"

Sally nodded her head eagerly, her soft, bright-red curls dancing around her freckled face. Sally's hair was not the same soft red as Annie's. It was closer to orange than red.

"You were just a little bitty girl when I left!"

Sally blushed. "I'm twelve years old now."

Jeremiah laughed and shook his head. "Have I been away that long?"

He put an arm around Sally's shoulders and approached the table, looking the food over. Annie thought he looked more Indian than white. The French and Indian blood that ran in his and Luke's veins from their grandparents certainly showed in both men, but Luke had those startlingly blue eyes.

"I can't believe that bunch of no-goods even left anything to eat," Jeremiah told Annie's mother. He sat down on the log, and Ethel began preparing a plate for him.

Annie walked to the other end of the table to cut another fresh pie, feeling nervous and wary. Luke kicked at another log, rolling it over near Jeremiah and turning it up on end to sit down. "You picked a damn good time to return," he told Jeremiah. "Just in time to be best man at my wedding."

Jeremiah's smile faded. He glanced at Annie, then looked at his brother. "Wedding?"

Luke nodded, and both men eyed each other almost challengingly for a moment.

"Let me guess," Jeremiah said. "Annie?"

"Yup."

At first, Annie thought some kind of trouble was brewing, but then Jeremiah put out his hand, shaking Luke's firmly. "Of course it's Annie. I'd have been surprised if it was anybody else. What the hell took you so long, brother?"

Luke laughed lightly. "Hell, she was only sixteen when you left, not quite old enough to be marrying yet. Besides, I wanted to build the farm up first, and build a proper house to bring her home to."

Jeremiah turned to look at the house again. "Well, you surely did that. Congratulations, brother. You're marrying the prettiest young woman and the best wife material in the Ohio Valley."

Annie brought the pie down closer to where Jeremiah sat. "Thank you, Jeremiah," she told him, hoping he understood the thanks was for more than the compliment. She was greatly relieved that the tension between the brothers had eased a bit. Jeremiah's attitude showed no animosity, no intention of making some kind of trouble over the upcoming nuptials. Still, when Jeremiah looked at her, she could see an appreciation in his eyes that spoke of more than friendship. Had he come back in hopes of finding that nothing romantic had come of her and Luke? How she wished they were alone. She wanted to scream at him, hit him . . . hug him. He was still handsome as ever, mysterious as ever.

He studied her lovingly for a moment, then turned back to his brother. "So, when will the wedding take place?"

"Less than two weeks," Luke answered. "You'll be here at least that long, won't you?"

Jeremiah shrugged. "Didn't plan on it, but since it's that close, sure, I'll stay. Got room in that fancy house for a wandering man, or would you rather I slept in one of your sheds?"

Luke rested his elbows on his knees. "You'll stay in the house, of course." He sobered. "And how about telling me the real reason you're here," he continued. "We do get news here, you know—a little old, but it comes. We know the war isn't near over."

Jeremiah swallowed half a biscuit. "No, it isn't. Let's not talk about the war right now, Luke. Looks like you've got quite an event going on here. You've got a barn to get built in a day. Why don't I help you do that and we can talk later."

Luke sighed. "All right. Just be careful what you say around some of the men. Not many here are in favor of going up against England, you know. Those that do are in for a bad time of it."

Jeremiah sobered. "You don't need to tell me that. I know firsthand." He looked at Annie again. "It's the biggest reason I didn't get back here sooner."

So, he was trying to explain something. Annie was filled with so many questions.

"Go ahead and finish eating," Luke told Jeremiah. He stood

up. "I agree it's best to get the barn finished first. As long as you're going to stay a while, we can talk later about where you've been and what you've been up to." He gave Jeremiah a playful punch on the shoulder and chuckled. "Mostly no good, I imagine." He walked around to Annie, grasping her hands and leaning down to kiss her cheek. "We'll all talk later." He squeezed her hands and left.

Once Luke was gone, Annie turned to Jeremiah, not sure if she should cry or be embarrassed or be angry. Mostly, she felt angry.

"You and I need to talk . . . alone," Jeremiah told her.

"Yes, we certainly do!" Annie turned away to hide the tears in her eyes.

"Annie."

She hesitated but did not face him.

"I'm so damned sorry . . . for everything. I'll explain more later. Just be assured you're marrying the right man, and I'm happy for both of you."

Annie swallowed back a lump in her throat and walked away.

3

The day dragged on, too hot as far as Annie was concerned. All around her came the sounds of women chatting, men shouting construction orders and sharing good-hearted jokes, the constant pounding of mauls, children screaming and laughing at play. Annie's head ached from the heat, mixed with the tension over Jeremiah's return. At least he'd said he was sorry. That was one small fact she could cling to, but it did little to ease her guilty conscience.

There came another round of meals for the men, then more work. Large support beams—most of them cut and grooved by Luke's own labor—were pounded and pegged into place; a rough plank roof, hand-grooved to overlap in order to ward off rain, was finished; and large, hinged doors were attached to each end of the sturdy barn. The day of laughter and visiting and hard work had grown dark by then, the men taking advantage of the late daylight hours of summer and working until nearly ten o'clock.

Because of the danger of traveling after dark, families stayed the night—some of them in the new barn, others out under the stars. Luke offered his house for Annie's family and Jeremiah, and finally everyone, hot and tired but feeling good about the

finished barn, sat down wearily in oak kitchen chairs handmade
by Luke. The chairs matched a large oak table, and a glance
around the central room of the sturdy stone house only told
Annie how much Luke loved her. This farm, this home, were
all for her, and they were things Jeremiah would likely never be
able to provide because of his preferred lifestyle. Annie began to
realize that could be part of the reason Jeremiah left, because he
knew Luke loved her and that Luke was better husband material. Still, to make love to her before leaving was unforgivable.
If Luke knew, surely he would want to kill Jeremiah, and would
probably never marry her.

The kitchen table sat before one of two large stone fireplaces
built into each end of the main room. The one at the kitchen
end had four built-in brick ovens, two on each side. Luke had
even built into it a chimney crane that a blacksmith at Fort
Harmar had made for him. From it hung several movable
wrought-iron arms from which Annie would be able to hang
cooking pots and swing out whichever pot was necessary, so that
she could check its contents away from the heat of the fire. No
one else in Willow Creek had such a luxurious cooking area. For
now, Annie heated a kettle of water for tea while the men re-
laxed. Jeremiah lit a small cigar and offered one to Luke.

"I prefer a pipe," Luke told him. He got up from the table
and walked over to a cowhide-covered, stuffed chair beside
which stood a smoking table in which he stored his tobacco and
pipes. He removed a pipe and stuffed it, talking while he did so.
"So, tell us where you've been." Finally, he'd asked Jeremiah the
question that was on everyone else's tongue.

Jeremiah ran a hand through his hair, still damp from washing his face and hands before coming inside. He took his cigar
from his mouth, and Annie set a tin bowl on the table where he
could rest the cigar. Their gazes met, and she told Jeremiah with

her look that she was probably more curious than anyone where Jeremiah had gone and what he'd been up to.

Before Jeremiah could answer, Annie's father spoke up. "Actually, I'd like to know when we can expect English soldiers to come snooping around here because of you," he told Jeremiah. "I have a feeling that you being here can't be good for us, son."

"Henry!" Ethel Barnes chastised her husband, a burly man who never minced words. "You haven't even given Jeremiah a chance to explain anything."

"It's all right," Jeremiah told Ethel.

"I'm sorry, Jeremiah, but some of the men were really grumbling out there today, especially John Hagan," Henry explained. "I don't trust that ornery, sour-faced son of—"

"Henry!" Ethel exclaimed again. "There are women present!"

Henry's barrel chest heaved in a sigh of resignation. "Well, I don't," he said. He scowled at Jeremiah. "Go ahead and tell us what's been going on."

Annie noticed her brothers and Sally leaning forward slightly, as though totally enraptured by Jeremiah's presence and hanging onto every word he spoke. She knew it surely irritated her father that Calvin and Jake now looked to Jeremiah as some kind of wandering hero who'd "been to war," and who might impress the young men into wanting to run off themselves.

Jeremiah leaned back in his chair. "I left Willow Creek because I decided someone needed to go and see what was going on with the English and colonials back East. I know you get news here, but it's old news by the time it arrives." He winced slightly and shifted in his chair. Annie noticed he seemed to favor his back.

"It didn't take long for me to see how right the Patriots are to risk their lives for freedom from England. I hunted up and spoke with George Washington himself, and when I left that meeting, I was ready to die for him, just like our own pa was willing to do. Washington respected him and mourned his death at Quebec. Our father fought for freedom from the horrors the French and Indians were visiting upon the colonists, and I intend to fight the same horrors the *English* are forcing on them!"

Annie and her family had never known Luke and Jeremiah's father, Noah. He'd been killed in 1759 at Quebec, fighting with the English against the French. According to both young men, Luke was only two then, Jeremiah five. Their heartbroken mother, Jess, never remarried. She and her grandfather raised and educated the boys in Albany, and when Jess Wilde died in 1769, Luke and Jeremiah headed West and landed at Willow Creek, where they befriended and lived part-time with Annie's family. Here, Luke began building his farm, but Jeremiah preferred to hunt for the settlers, which was how he'd become acquainted with some of the area's Delaware Indians.

"I ended up involved in the fighting," Jeremiah continued.

"Of course you did," Luke answered. "I wouldn't expect anything less of you." He walked over to the fireplace and grabbed hold of the unburned end of a kindling stick. "That doesn't mean you couldn't have put a pen to paper and written home," he added with a hint of anger. He held the burning end of the stick to his pipe bowl and drew on the pipe to light it.

Jeremiah frowned at his brother, and Annie could feel a growing tension between them. "No, it doesn't, but Washington put me in charge of helping train new recruits, and when you are moving all over the country training an army made up of men who hardly know the butt end of a musket from the barrel end, it isn't easy to find the time to write, let alone finding someone willing to bring letters all the way back here. You know yourself that most of your news comes from suppliers who come here only once or twice a year. To send someone special with one man's letter is next to impossible."

Luke nodded. "All right. I'll grant you it would have been hard to keep in touch with us." He took another draw on the pipe. "So what brings you here now? We're all pretty sure the fighting isn't over. Why did you leave it to come home?"

Jeremiah rubbed at his eyes. "Because my brother is here." His gaze landed on Annie for just a moment, then moved to the rest of her family. "And other people I care about. When I escaped a prison ship and learned that George Washington had been appointed President of the new United States, I figured things were going well enough to come home for a while. I—"

"Wait! Wait! Wait a minute!" Luke interrupted. "Go back a bit, brother. When you escaped *what?*"

"Are you being hunted, Jeremiah Wilde?" Henry Barnes asked.

Annie's heart pounded with fear for Jeremiah.

"Probably," Jeremiah answered.

Luke rolled his eyes. "I knew there was more to this than meets the eye."

"Don't worry," Jeremiah added. "The English are looking all over New York for me. I have friends in the right places, and people are telling them they've seen me there and think I'm hiding out in the city. None of them even know where I've really gone."

"But some of them know where you're *from,* right?" Luke asked.

"They won't say a thing."

"You can't count on that!"

Jeremiah scooted back his chair and rose, leaving his cigar in the tin dish. He walked to the fireplace, stretching out his arm and bracing it against the mantle. "I doubt I'm important enough for the English to send men this far looking for me," he told Luke. "Right now, they aren't concerned with remote areas like this. They figure Indian raids out here will take care of any Patriots who might live this far west, and they don't mind bribing the Indians to take care of such matters, so you all need to be more on guard than ever. Don't forget that the Ohio Valley was supposed to be left for the Indians, who aren't happy about these settlements on their land. With so much trouble going on, I figured the best place to lay low would be right here, because I was worried about all of you. You just might need an extra hand."

"So, you're not going back East?" Henry asked.

Jeremiah began pacing. "I don't know right now. I only know I won't give up the fight. George Washington is carrying this cause almost completely on his shoulders, from commanding the Continental Army to being President. He needs all the help he can get, and now we at least have France on our side."

"*France!*" Luke exclaimed. "That's the very country our father fought *against!*"

"Given the circumstances, he'd be just as adamant about fighting the English now," Jeremiah answered. "Besides, he'd be ready and willing to help Washington if he were alive today. You know that."

Luke frowned and turned away, shaking his head.

"Things change, Luke," Jeremiah told him. "England is the enemy now. If the colonists don't stand up for themselves and declare independence, England will keep on reaping the harvest of lumber and raw materials and our farm produce, and the colonists will be left starving and owing too many taxes! The king doesn't give a damn about what people are suffering over here, as long as he can profit from what we have to offer. People like you will work themselves into the ground for *England,* not for their own future and the future of their children. We'll all forever be *slaves* to England if we don't do something about it. You can abuse people for just so long, until the time comes when they won't *take* it anymore!"

Annie silently set a can of tea leaves on the table, hating the argument, loving both men, dreading where the conversation might go. She swallowed nervously when Jeremiah stepped even closer to Luke, facing him squarely—two men of equal height and stature, and strength.

"And don't blame *me* for leaving and getting involved," Jeremiah added, more quietly this time. "I left for *your* sake, remember? I left because it was the right thing to do."

The two men's gazes held for several long, silent seconds, and Annie couldn't help wondering what Jeremiah meant by the remark. Luke closed his eyes and sighed. "I remember," he answered, turning away. He stared at the fire, drawing on his pipe again.

"We all know there is a war going on and the reasons why," Henry told Jeremiah. "I guess we've been hoping it wouldn't come to us, clear out here. And for God's sake, Jeremiah, you're talking about inexperienced farmers going up against the mightiest power in the world!"

"I know that." Jeremiah turned from watching his brother. "I never thought I would get this involved myself, but I am, and that's the hell of it."

"Tell us about escaping, Jeremiah," Jake asked, obvious excitement in his voice. "Were you in some kind of prison?"

Dark hatred came into Jeremiah's eyes. "You could call it that. Actually, it was worse than prison." He sat down again, this time gingerly, as though in pain. "I was in a meeting with about twenty other Patriots in a man's barn in New York when English soldiers burst in and arrested all of us. We'll probably never know who betrayed us, but the man who owned the barn was branded the instigator of the meeting and was hanged on the spot, in his own barn."

Ethel gasped and put a hand to her mouth.

"They decided to use the rest of us as an example for other Patriots," Jeremiah continued. "They paraded us through the streets of New York and let Loyalists throw garbage and rocks at us. Two men were actually stoned to death. The rest of us were taken to the shipping docks and broken up into smaller groups, then put onto various English merchant ships to be used like slaves to swab the decks and help with rowing when the wind was still. We cooked, cleaned chamber pots, spittoons, and the like. We were half-starved, and English deckhands were allowed to ridicule us."

"Good God," Luke muttered.

Annie ached for Jeremiah.

"Any man who refused his duties was tied to a mast and whipped up to thirty lashes, sometimes more."

Luke closed his eyes. "And knowing you, you refused, probably more than once."

Jeremiah stared at the cigar in the tin dish. "I refused, but not more than once. My back couldn't have taken another lashing without baring my spine and killing me. I'm lucky to be walking, and I still have back trouble because of it. Sometime when the women aren't present, I'll show you my back."

Annie felt sick.

"Dear God," Ethel muttered, covering her eyes.

"You should have said something," Luke told him. "I wouldn't have asked you to help with the barn."

"I would have helped anyway. I sure as hell owe you that much. Maybe now you better understand my hatred for the English," Jeremiah told them. "This war will last a lot longer, but the Patriots, in spite of how they are suffering right now, will prevail. I truly believe that. They have already won several important offensives. I took part in one of them in seventy-six, when I first arrived in the East. I helped defend the lines around Boston that eventually forced the English General Howe to vacate the city. That particular battle left the new Continental Army with two hundred fifty English cannon to use for their war. That got my excitement going. We *are* going to win this, Luke. There is nothing wrong with wanting independence."

"I never said that was wrong," Luke told Jeremiah. "I just fear it's a lost cause. The more we resist, the more innocents will suffer. The British have highly trained soldiers and all kinds of money and power behind them. What do we have?"

Jeremiah looked up at him. "Determination," he answered. "And hatred. And I believe God is on our side." He turned to Henry. "I wanted to come here and warn you not to let down your guard." He glanced at Annie, then Luke. "Especially now that you're getting married. You and Annie will be out here alone on this farm, away from the settlement."

Luke nodded. "We'll be careful, and I've fought off my share of Indians. Right now, I'd say the one in the most danger is you. How did you escape that ship?"

Jeremiah leaned forward, resting his elbows on his knees. "I was in the ship's hold with some other prisoners when I caught the guard half asleep. I, uh ... strangled him ... and stole his keys."

"Good Lord, now we add murder to this mess!" Luke groaned.

"You would have done the same thing to get out of there," Jeremiah told him. "I and several others escaped and swam to shore. My connections in New York gave me refuge until I could get my strength back and put on a little weight. They also provided me with money, weapons, clothes, and a horse. I headed this way and never stopped." He scanned the others at the table. "Look, it's late, and we're all very tired. I don't know about the rest of you, but I'm going outside to open my bedroll and get some sleep. We can talk more about this tomorrow."

"You don't have to sleep outside," Luke told him.

"I don't mind. I've been mostly sleeping on the ground or in a ship's hold for a long time. Besides, believe it or not, the hard ground feels better on my back. You have Annie's whole family to put up for the night. Once everyone goes home, I'll stay on here and help out with the farm until the wedding. That will give you and me some time to catch up."

"Fine." Luke, who also appeared bone-weary, walked over to stand behind Jeremiah. He squeezed his shoulders. "I'm glad you survived and got away from that ship."

Jeremiah stood up and faced his brother. "And I'm glad things are going so well for you." The brothers shook hands firmly again, and Jeremiah turned to the others. "I'll see all of you in the morning."

"Good night, Jeremiah. I will pray for your safety," Ethel told him.

Jeremiah nodded to her. "Thank you." He glanced at Annie once more, then turned and left.

Henry shook his head. "Quite a turn of events," he told the others. "I'm sorry for your brother, Luke, and I hope we don't see any of that trouble Jeremiah talked about." He, too, stood up. "Where do you want us to sleep?"

"Doesn't anyone want tea?" Annie asked. "I never even had the chance to fix some for you."

"I'd just as soon turn in," Henry told her.

Luke nodded toward a balcony that spanned the length of the house, the railing made of pine poles. Behind it were two extra bedrooms, *for our big family* Luke had told Annie not long ago.

"You and Ethel can sleep in one of the rooms upstairs, and Annie and Sally can sleep in the other," Luke told Henry. "I'll sleep down here with the boys in the third bedroom."

"Fine." Henry smiled at Luke, putting a hand on his arm. "You've a fine home here, Luke."

Luke nodded his thanks. "I'm sorry for the worry Jeremiah has caused."

"He's your brother, and we love him the same as you," Henry told him. He motioned for Ethel to join him and they both wearily climbed the varnished stairs made of logs cut in half lengthwise.

Annie thought how much her mother had aged lately, her red hair heavily streaked with gray. Ethel Barnes was a tall, graceful, uncomplaining woman of deep faith who went about her daily chores with literal joy. Annie hoped to be just like her. She walked up to Luke. "You look so tired. How can I possibly explain what all your hard work means to me, Luke? The farm . . . this beautiful house . . ."

He smiled, leaning down to kiss her cheek. "Before long, I'll have all the thanks I need," he said, adding, "when you become my wife." He glanced up to be sure her parents had gone into their room, then met her lips in a quick but suggestive kiss that stirred a desire she'd once held for his brother. She and Jeremiah had lain together just that one night, but she'd not forgotten the ecstasy of sharing her body with a man. Soon she would experience that again . . . with Luke.

"Luke kissed Annie!" Sally shouted up to her parents.

Luke chuckled, and Annie scowled at her sister. "Sally Barnes!"

Quickly, Luke planted one last kiss on Annie's forehead, then went after Sally as though to scold her. Sally screamed and raced up the stairs. Annie laughed and followed, then stopped to look back at Luke. "I love you," she told him.

"And I love you." Luke turned to Jake and Calvin. "Come on, boys. I'll show you where to sleep." He disappeared into one of the downstairs bedrooms, and Annie glanced at a front window, wondering when she and Jeremiah would be able to have that much-needed talk. Maybe they shouldn't talk at all. Maybe it was best to let the past lie in the past. Still, she'd loved him desperately once, so much so that she'd committed the worst sin a young girl could commit. There was no taking it back now.

4

Annie ached from a long day followed by lack of sleep. All
night long she worried over Jeremiah's return, the dangers
he would face if and when he went back East, the possible trou-
bles Willow Creek might be facing, the upcoming wedding.
There were so many things to think about, and there was still
her own guilty conscience to deal with. That she could have lived
with . . . if only Jeremiah had not come back.

She rose and dressed even before the rooster crowed, using
the soft light of a lantern she'd turned low before retiring. Need-
ing to keep busy, she quietly washed her face and hands using
the bowl and pitcher Luke had been thoughtful enough to set
out in the bedroom, then removed her nightcap and brushed
back her hair. She twisted it into a bun at the base of her neck
and fastened it with a comb.

On stockinged feet, she headed down the stairs and began
searching through the cupboards for items with which to make
biscuits and gravy for breakfast. She wanted to feed her family
before heading back to Willow Creek. She managed to find a
lidded can filled with flour, and she couldn't help thinking how
badly Luke's kitchen needed rearranging to make it more con-
venient for a woman. In the pantry board she found some butter

she'd churned herself for Luke and brought along for the barn raising.

She dug through a lower cupboard looking for a mixing bowl, and when she rose and turned, Luke came through the front door.

"Luke!" She set the bowl on the table, speaking softly so as not to disturb the others. "I had no idea you were up, too."

He smiled, his blue eyes showing love, but also a strange sadness. "I've been outside talking to Jeremiah. He couldn't sleep either." He sighed as though greatly burdened. "I'm worried about him, Annie . . . and about what could happen around here. We've put the war to the back of our minds, but Jeremiah's return has made me more aware of what's going on back East."

Annie stepped closer, moving her arms around his waist. "I know how you're feeling."

Luke embraced her in return, pressing her close. "Annie, I know you need to talk to Jeremiah alone."

Annie felt a tingling in every nerve. "What?"

Luke grasped her arms and pushed her away slightly, still speaking quietly so the others wouldn't hear. "I mean, you loved him once, and the way he left, so suddenly, must have left a lot of questions in your mind."

Annie felt a flush coming to her cheeks, and she wanted to cry. Her heart pounded with dread. What did he know? "Luke, I love *you!*"

"I know that. I'm just telling you that I understand there might be things the two of you need to talk about. I've never brought this up, Annie, because I knew you needed time to get over Jeremiah; and then it seemed that maybe he'd never even come back. But he has, and when he left . . . you don't know it, but he and I fought over you."

"Luke!"

"It's all right. It was three years ago, and we were all younger. Jeremiah came to tell me he was leaving and said it was because he loved you, something I didn't even expect. He knew *I* loved you, too, and that I had already made up my mind to marry you someday. I landed into him before he even had a chance to explain that he was leaving for my sake. He's not the kind of man to ever settle for long, or to stay home with a wife and children and work on a farm. He's always been that way. And he loved you—and me—enough to just leave, hoping you and I would end up together. Now I owe it to both of you to let you talk alone. Jeremiah already told me he wants to speak to you."

Annie felt consumed by guilt as she studied the sincerity in Luke's handsome blue eyes. He was a man of such honor and integrity ... and he loved her far beyond what she deserved. Now it was also obvious how much he loved Jeremiah, and how much he trusted both of them.

"Luke, that's all in the past. I didn't even realize you knew." Now tears began to fill her eyes. "Luke, please don't think—"

"I don't think anything. I saw the hurt in your eyes after Jeremiah left, Annie. That's why I stayed away that first year, but it hurt me, too. Then after I started seeing you, and I saw love come into those pretty green eyes ..." He studied her lovingly. "I've loved you for a long time, Annie. I'll always be here for you."

"I know you will." Her hands shaking, Annie wiped at the tears on her cheeks. Should she tell him? No. She would talk to Jeremiah first. She grasped Luke's arms, thinking how hard-muscled they were. This man was all of Jeremiah and more. He was just as handsome, and so much more dependable ... and so understanding. Then again, if he knew the whole truth ... "Luke, I love you in ways I never could have loved Jeremiah.

I'll be so proud to be your wife. You should have told me you knew!" Tears ran down her cheeks. "You should have let me explain." She met his gaze with a pleading look. "Tell me you don't hate Jeremiah. And please don't argue anymore while he's here."

"I don't hate him, and no, we won't argue. Actually, I'm glad to see him again and know that he's all right. I was feeling guilty for being almost completely responsible for his leaving. If he'd been killed—"

"I was feeling the same guilt!" Annie told him. "I'm so glad you understand why I'm also relieved that he's all right. I didn't know what to think or do when he came back, and I didn't know what *you* were thinking."

Luke grasped her face, wiping at more tears with his thumbs. "I was thinking how glad I am that three years have gone by and you're mine now." He leaned close, tasting her mouth, a light kiss turning into something much deeper, much more suggestive. Annie reached around his neck, and he pulled her closer, crushing her against him as the kiss turned even more delicious and heated. Luke moved his lips to her eyes, her cheek, her neck. Passion and desire ripped through Annie's insides, and she knew that her wedding night with this man would be nothing but pleasure and fulfillment.

Finally, Luke pulled away, clearing his throat and actually looking a little flushed. He took a deep breath. "Well now, I expect our wedding can't come any too soon, can it?"

Now it was Annie's turn to blush. She laughed lightly, sniffling back lingering tears. "No, it can't."

He turned away from her. "Go on outside and talk to Jeremiah. He's sitting on the porch."

"You're sure it's all right?"

He turned his head and looked her over lovingly. "I wouldn't be marrying you if I wasn't."

Annie reached out and squeezed his hand, then turned and walked to the front door, stepping out into the light of dawn and finally hearing the rooster crow for the first time that morning. There sat Jeremiah on the steps. She closed the door and he looked up at her with dark eyes that showed an alarming weariness.

"You've got to get more rest," Annie told him.

"I will." His gaze moved over her lovingly. "You're more beautiful than when I left; more womanly."

The remark came unexpectedly, and Annie looked away, somewhat embarrassed. "God knows what a foolish child I was three years ago."

Jeremiah rubbed at his eyes. "Yeah, well, I didn't have much sense either, did I?" With a deep sigh that spelled regret, he stood up, taking her arm and leading her down the steps and around to the side of the house. He sat down on a small wooden bench, motioning for Annie to sit down beside him. For a few silent seconds, they just sat there, each waiting for the other to speak.

"Quite a place Luke has built up here," Jeremiah finally said. He faced Annie. "It's all for you, you know."

Annie looked at her lap. "I know."

Jeremiah reached over and enfolded her hand in his own. "I'm so sorry, Annie, for taking advantage of your feelings and then just leaving like that. I can't imagine what you think of me."

The hurt ran so deep. "No, you can't," she answered quietly, fighting new tears. She pulled her hand away. "Nor can *I* imagine what you think of *me*. I'm hardly worthy to be marrying an honorable man like your brother." She heard him give out an odd snicker.

"You damned well *are* worthy, and don't you ever doubt

that! It's *me* who's not worthy to be *called* his brother." He turned away. "Jesus," he muttered.

"Don't use the Lord's name in vain."

"Well now, God knows that would be one of the *least* of my sins, doesn't He?"

A lump rose in Annie's throat to painful proportions, and she couldn't speak.

Jeremiah sighed. "Annie, I'm the one at fault here. I'm the *only* one at fault. *I* betrayed Luke, not you. You weren't in love with him then, but I knew he cared about you, and I knew he was the better man for you. I took advantage of your feelings anyway. Luke is a good man, and he loves you dearly. And if you think I'd ever say anything to him about what happened, you're wrong. I would never hurt him like that, but what I did . . . it was selfish. I knew damn well I wasn't the man for you, but I . . . loved you. I wanted you. And I decided that if I was going to give you up forever, I had to have you . . . just once. I'll never forgive myself for that."

Annie swallowed and forced her voice to come forward. "Did you give one thought to the position you might have left me in? My God, Jeremiah, you could have left me carrying! I could have been forever branded, and the child would have been called a bastard!"

He faced her and grasped her hands. "You didn't—"

"No, thank God!" Finally, she managed to turn to him, looking into those dark, handsome eyes, studying the wildness about him. "Yes, it *was* selfish, Jeremiah. I truly loved you. Surely you knew how devastated I would be when you left like that. I cried alone at night for weeks. During the day, I had to hide the awful pain, because no one would have understood why it ran so deep." Now the tears came, and she looked away. "I've been so ashamed ever since." She jerked in a sob. "And I've felt so . . . unworthy of Luke . . . and of all the wonderful things he's done for me."

Jeremiah squeezed her hands. "Look at me, Annie."

Shivering with tears, she met his gaze again. "Luke loves you in ways I never could. I didn't love you enough to give up the way I wanted to live. I didn't love you enough to stay here and provide a proper home for you. But I did love you, Annie. Fact is, I still do. A little piece of me hoped you'd still be free when I got back, but the rest of me knows it wouldn't have mattered. I have a damn good idea Luke would love you and marry you even if he knew what happened between us, but it's because I care about him that I'll never tell him, and I don't want you to tell him either. I couldn't stand the hurt he'd feel over my betrayal. From here on, I want you to consider that it never happened. And no matter what else, it was all *my* fault, not yours. I want you to let yourself be happy with Luke. It won't be easy for me to watch you marry him, but that's how it has to be. I knew Luke would seek you out and eventually voice his feelings for you. And I knew he couldn't find a better woman in the Ohio Valley."

Her tears dripped on his hands. "I was afraid you had just . . . used me . . . and perhaps laughed about it later."

"Oh, Annie, surely you know me better than that! We were longtime friends before we were lovers."

Lovers. Yes, they had been lovers. "I still love you, Jeremiah. I always will, but not the way I love Luke now."

Jeremiah nodded. "That's okay." He moved an arm around her, and she rested her head on his shoulder and wept. "Annie, I want you to remember one thing. If anything should ever happen to Luke, you seek me out. I'll try to always let the two of you know where I am. I'll come here and I'll take care of you like Luke would have. If you have children, I'll take them in as my own. I'll always love you, Annie. I don't ever want you to feel bad about what happened between us."

Annie pulled a handkerchief from a pocket on her dress and wiped at her eyes and nose. "That's all I need to hear, Jeremiah." She sat straighter and breathed deeply for self-control. She met his gaze, and in spite of his brash wildness and wandering ways, she was amazed to detect tears in his eyes, eyes that could capture and mesmerize a person, eyes that could also show cunning and stealth. Yes, this man truly belonged in the wilds, and from what she'd heard of his father, that character was bred in him. She wondered if the same wildness might show itself in Luke someday. She hoped not.

"I want you to forgive me, Annie."

She had to look away again and wipe at more tears. "I forgive you, Jeremiah," she whispered.

He pressed her shoulder. "You'll be happy with Luke."

She nodded. "I know I will." She sniffled. "What about you? Will you ever be happy, Jeremiah?"

He smiled sadly. "All I need is my musket, a tomahawk, and a good smoke to be happy."

"You can't wander your whole life."

He shrugged. "Some men do."

"Maybe you'll marry an Indian woman someday."

He looked out at Luke's cornfields. "Maybe. I don't think much about such things right now. All I can think about is winning this war. I'll worry about my personal life after that. For now, I'll stay here long enough to have a good visit with my brother and stand up for him at your wedding. Then I'll be on my way. I figured to stay around Willow Creek for a while in case of trouble, but . . . I think it's best I don't stay too close after you and Luke are married. It's best I leave. Besides, the settlement has grown some. There should be enough men in town to defend it pretty well. Still, I'll worry, especially with you and Luke clear out here away from town."

"And we will worry about you."

He turned to her with a reassuring smile. "That's one thing you don't have to do. I can take care of myself just fine. I've been in scrapes most men would never survive, but I always manage to come through all right."

She smiled through tears. "Yes, you do, don't you?"

In the distance, the rooster crowed once more. Jeremiah sighed, looking out at the cornfield again. "It's so peaceful here right now. I hope it stays that way."

Annie nodded. "Don't we all?"

Jeremiah faced her. "War can change a lot of things, Annie. I pray to God you and Luke never get tested."

His words frightened her. "We love each other enough to survive anything."

His gaze moved over her lovingly. "I expect you do." He sighed and rose. "We'd better get inside. It wouldn't look good to stay out here too long." He reached out his hand, and Annie took it. Jeremiah pulled her to her feet, then looked around before leaning down to kiss her lightly. "God go with you, Annie Barnes."

So handsome. So lonely. So easy to love . . . and so hard to forget. "And with you, Jeremiah Wilde. A piece of my heart will always be with you."

He smiled. "And I will hold on to it with the deepest respect and gratefulness." He squeezed her hand once more. "I don't plan on seeing you again till your wedding day. I do intend to hunt down a nice, fattened buck to roast that day for your wedding feast. That will be my gift to you and Luke."

"It's a splendid gift."

They stood there a moment longer, each knowing full well they would not mind a last embrace, a last lingering kiss, both realizing it would be wrong. Jeremiah let go of her hand. "Bye, Annie. I'm sorry I never even stopped to say that much the first time I left."

She laughed, a laugh of sorrow that was followed by a quick, deep sob. "So am I." She turned away. "Good-bye, Jeremiah."

"Annie—"

"Go! Just go! Please wait until my family and I leave for town before you come back, will you?"

He touched her shoulder. "Whatever you want. Thanks for coming out to talk with me."

Annie heard only silence then. Finally, she turned to see he was gone. She realized then that he could move as silently as an Indian. He seemed to blow in and out of her life like a quick wind, and this quick good-bye seemed too short, after not seeing him for three whole years. Still, there was nothing more to be said between them except "I love you," and "I'm sorry."

She took a moment to lean against the house and let more tears come. She had to get them out before going back inside to face Luke and her family. "God protect him," she wept.

5

Annie breathed deeply as she approached the crowd waiting outside the little Methodist chapel, a log structure built only last year by Preacher Falls. People sometimes came from many miles around on special religious holidays just to hear Preacher Falls's sermons, or to witness and celebrate a wedding, or even a baptism.

Today they were here to witness her marriage to Luke. Her stomach fluttered, and she felt short of breath from nervousness. As Jeremiah had promised, she'd not seen him since the morning they talked after the barn raising.

She chided herself for wanting to look pretty for both brothers. She'd worked on her light green linen dress for weeks, thrilled to find the pretty material among goods brought to Willow Creek from the East last summer. With all the problems over the revolution, the merchant who'd brought the supplies told them it was a miracle he'd made it through at all, and so far this year, no traders had come.

Annie felt proud of her ability with needle and thread. The

dress was fitted at the waist over a tightly drawn corset. Flowered embroidery decorated a cascading trim from waist to hem, and the three-quarter-length sleeves were trimmed with three-inch white lace and dark green ribbon. Over the bodice of the dress and attached under the white collar, she wore a cape of white lace tied with the same dark green ribbon that trimmed her sleeves; and over her hair, which hung in long sausage curls, she wore a mobcap of sheer white lawn trimmed in ruffles of white lace. She carried a bouquet of wild yellow-and-orange tiger lilies her sister had found growing along the Ohio River.

Beside her walked her mother and father, followed by Sally, Jake, and Calvin. As they came closer, the crowd parted, everyone smiling and making comments about how beautiful she looked. After the wedding, they would all feast royally on a deer carcass currently roasting over an open pit. Jeremiah had hunted, skinned, and dressed out the deer as his wedding gift, another promise he'd kept.

Annie pinched her cheeks once more to bring more color to them, then drew a deep breath to stave off the jitters. Not only was she nervous about Jeremiah being here, but she was keenly aware that this would be her wedding night with Luke. She felt both excitement and apprehension at the thought of lying with him.

Ethel kept an arm around her as they walked up the two steps of the small stoop at the front door of the chapel. They stopped there, and Ethel and Annie's siblings were escorted inside by Jenny Carlson's brother Clete. Annie stood watching the front of the chapel as her family was seated. There stood Jeremiah next to Luke. *God help me stay calm,* she thought.

Jeremiah wore homespun dark brown britches, white knee-high stockings, and dark leather shoes decorated with buckles. His drop-shoulder white shirt was open at the neck, and over it he wore a long, dark-brown leather vest buttoned at the waist-line. It seemed strange to see him standing there weaponless and in simple attire. His long hair was pulled straight back into a tail at the neck, revealing his dark-skinned, finely chiseled face. He watched her for a moment with a look of love and reassurance, then glanced away.

Beside him stood his very handsome brother. Luke! How fine he looked! Annie had never seen him dressed the way he was today. In fact, no one in Willow Creek had ever dressed so splendidly, and where and when he had managed to get such a suit, she could not imagine. It was dark-blue satin, a beautiful color against his so-blue eyes. The suit was trimmed with silver buttons down the front and at the wide, turned-up cuffs of the jacket. Under the jacket he wore a lighter blue waistcoat covered with fancy embroidery, and at the neck, a ruffled cravat. The knee-length britches buttoned just under the knees with the same silver buttons that decorated his suit coat, the rest of his legs covered by white stockings. His black-leather shoes displayed large tongues trimmed with silver buckles, a style she was sure only wealthy men wore.

And Luke was, indeed, wealthy, at least by pioneer standards. She was marrying a good, solid, settled man any woman would want. She breathed deeply, knowing with relief that she'd made the right choice. She must concentrate today only on Luke. She kept her eyes on him as people stood up, and Hilda Pickens played a lovely song on the piano, the only musical instrument in the entire village besides a couple of fiddles. Henry Barnes took hold of his daughter's arm and began walking her down the short aisle to where Luke stood waiting, his blue eyes literally glittering with love and pride as he looked her over.

Annie could feel Jeremiah's presence, felt him looking at her as she kept her eyes averted. *Watch Luke,* she reminded herself

again. *Watch only Luke*. She felt removed from the occasion as
the preacher said something about whether or not anyone ob-
jected to this marriage—"Speak now or forever hold his peace."

Would Jeremiah speak up? Of course not. He loved his
brother. He knew the best thing to do was to let her marry Luke.

"Who gives this woman to be married to this man?"

She heard her father answer, "I do."

Now it was Luke who took her hand, enfolding it warmly
in his own. Luke. So strong. So rock-solid, both physically and
emotionally. So supportive. So committed. She hadn't seen him
for the past six days. He'd deliberately stayed away to make this
day more exciting for both of them.

They spoke their vows, feeling more love as they watched
each other's eyes than they'd ever felt before. In minutes, it was
over. She was pronounced Mrs. Luke Wilde. Luke leaned down
and kissed her lightly, but the look in his eyes told her there was
much more to come once they were alone. She was not afraid or
even nervous anymore, only anxious. Luke put an arm around
her and they greeted a few people as they walked outside, where
friends clapped and hugged them, giving them their wishes for
happiness and health and wealth.

Everyone came out of the church, and Jeremiah walked up
to Luke, shaking his hand. "You picked the finest woman in the
valley," he told Luke. "I'm happy for you."

Luke laughed, shaking his brother's hand vigorously in return. "I wish you'd settle down yourself, brother," he answered.
"I'll miss you when you're gone."

Jeremiah glanced at Annie. "Maybe someday," he said. He
leaned down and kissed her cheek. "Congratulations, sister-in-
law," he told her, smiling.

"Thank you, Jeremiah," she answered sincerely. She moved
her arm around Luke's waist, hugging him close. He leaned

down and kissed her again, and others began congratulating them, shaking Luke's hand and hugging Annie; but suddenly the mood of the crowd changed, and women began screaming. The crowd broke up and backed away as a troop of English soldiers charged down the narrow dirt street, sabers clanking against other weapons. They halted in front of the wedding party, horses panting and lathered.

Pain exploded in Annie's chest as terror filled her, and Luke pushed her behind him protectively.

"What is this?" Luke demanded.

"We are looking for Jeremiah Wilde!" the leader of the troop shouted. He yanked his sword from its sheath and waved it in the air. "Produce him now or suffer the consequences!"

Women gasped and people whispered among themselves, no one anxious to give over the groom's brother, especially on this day of celebration.

Annie's heart pounded with fear and dread. *Jeremiah!* How had they traced him to Willow Creek? Did they know him by sight? If not, would anyone here betray his presence? Luke grasped her closer, and Annie glanced over to where Jeremiah had been standing. He was gone!

The lead soldier rode even closer on a sturdy white horse, lowering his sword to rest it on Luke's shoulder. "And what might *your* name be?"

6

Fear engulfed Annie. Not only were these soldiers most likely here to kill Jeremiah, but now the man in charge rested his sword on Luke's shoulder, insinuating he could slice off his head at any moment! Luke in turn faced the English soldier with unflinching stubbornness. "My name is *Luke* Wilde," he answered boldly.

The crowd around them quieted, most likely waiting for Luke's lead in what they should do or say.

"Wilde, is it?" The soldier grinned. "How interesting. And from your build, I am guessing you might be Jeremiah Wilde's brother. Am I right?"

"You might find it easier to talk to me if you take your damn sword off my shoulder! I don't intend to see blood spilled on my wedding day, nor in front of my wife."

The Englishman chuckled, removing the sword but not sheathing it. "And aren't you quite the fashionable groom?" He looked around at the others warily, then back at Luke. "You apparently are one of the wealthier pilgrims in this excuse for a settlement, just as your father and grandfather were decently well-off back in Albany."

Luke frowned. "How do you know about them?"

The Englishman's eyes twinkled with delight in having the upper hand. "The king expects us to know everything we can about his American subjects. Besides, English officers in Albany tell me that Noah Wilde left behind quite a reputation as a defender of England in the French and Indian War."

"All the more reason to treat his sons with respect!"

"Hmmmm, perhaps. Isn't it interesting how tables can turn? Your father fought with the colonists against the French back then, and now the French are helping all of you fight the English. What an odd twist of fate. And what a foolish decision on the part of the American subjects to think they can be independent. What is *your* feeling on the subject, Mr. Wilde?"

Luke folded his arms. "I don't really have an opinion yet. Your behavior here certainly doesn't help sway me to the Loyalist side."

The soldier leaned closer. "And the fact that you are Jeremiah Wilde's brother does not help sway *me* against running a sword through your heart this very moment!" he growled. "If he is here, you had best tell me now where I can find him, before my men and I destroy this settlement looking for him!"

"How dare you come here and threaten us this way!" Preacher Falls cried out.

"Leave it alone, Preacher," Luke ordered him as some of the other soldiers, still on horseback, spread out to surround the crowd.

"Make swords ready!" their leader commanded.

In one synchronized movement, the others pulled their swords and held them at their sides, pointed straight up.

"You could at least tell us your name and rank," Luke told their leader, still glaring at him.

The Englishman straightened proudly. "I am Richard Weatherford, Esquire—Sir Richard to simple people like yourself, Colonel Weatherford to the men who ride with me."

"Well, *Sir* Richard, surely you pride yourself in being a gentleman. Your behavior here on my wedding day defies any hint of that. As you can see, my brother is not here. He left three years ago. I am well aware of his capabilities at hiding, sometimes even among the Indians, so if you can't find him, that is your problem, not ours. This is a peaceful settlement, and not one occupant here has raised a hand against the English. You can take your search someplace else."

Weatherford shook his head. "When it comes to war, I assure you, Luke Wilde, that I care little about being a gentleman to the enemy. Jeremiah Wilde is a traitor to the Crown. He has killed British subjects, one of them while escaping imprisonment on a British frigate. That, Mr. Wilde, is not an act of war. That is murder! Your brother is a fugitive. And just as your father was dangerous to the French, your brother is dangerous to the *British!* I have been assigned to find him, and since often a man's first choice when fleeing the law is to try to reach his family, I came here to look for him. Now, I will repeat, tell me if you have seen him and if you know where he is, or I will tear this village apart!"

Annie shivered behind Luke.

"I have *not* seen him," Luke lied, still refusing to back down.

Weatherford again placed his sword on Luke's shoulder. "And I think you are *lying!*"

"Stop it!" Annie cried, stepping forward. "He's told you the truth!"

Luke grabbed her arm. "Damn it, Annie, stay behind me! I'll handle this!" He started to shove her behind him again, but in an instant, the tip of Weatherford's sword rested against her breast.

"Stay where you are!" Weatherford ordered Annie. He

looked at Luke. "If I have to use your wench to get the truth out of you, I'll do it!"

"Remove your sword from that woman or die!"

Annie was stunned to hear Jeremiah's voice. He emerged from between two buildings, holding a musket to his shoulder and aimed directly at Weatherford. "Killing one more Englishman won't bother me one bit!"

Annie's eyes quickly filled with tears of terror. Surely Jeremiah would die before her eyes today, and maybe Luke also, for lying to the Redcoats!

Weatherford took his sword from Annie and sheathed it. "Well, well, well," the colonel said, grinning. He turned his horse to face Jeremiah. "Was it the threat to your brother that brought you out of hiding, or to his wench?"

"It's your threat to this whole village! I'll not allow innocent blood to be shed for my sake!"

"Ah!" Weatherford grasped his sword hilt. "Jeremiah Wilde, I take it."

"I am Jeremiah."

Weatherford grinned. "Well then, why not make this a bloodless day, in honor of your brother's marriage, and put your musket down? There is no sense in shooting me, Mr. Wilde, as the rest of my men will finish you off before you can have a fair trial in Albany."

"A fair trial? Do you really expect me to believe that will happen?"

"The king has ordered it, only because of the help the English received from your father against the French."

"I can't believe you won't kill my brother before you reach Albany!" Luke put in, stepping closer to Weatherford, fists clenched.

"Luke, be careful!" Annie told him.

"Stay out of this, Luke!" Jeremiah pleaded.

"I'm already involved! This tyrant dared to touch his sword to my *wife!* Let alone the fact that he called her a wench!"

The colonel whirled his horse and urged it forward so quickly that it knocked Luke down. Annie and other women screamed as a shot rang out and a lead ball ripped across Weatherford's shoulder, then nicked his chin. The man cried out, and at the same time, another shot was fired.

Everything happened so quickly that Annie wasn't even sure at first of every event. She only knew that Luke and Weatherford lay on the ground, and then Luke was up again, shoving Weatherford's horse backward. It was then he and Annie both noticed that Jeremiah was also down, and bleeding from his side. Several soldiers stood over him, rifles pointed at him.

"Bastards!" Luke cried out. He stormed across to Jeremiah and paid no heed to the soldiers as he bent over him. "Jeremiah!"

"The sonofabitch shot me!" Weatherford cried. He got to his feet, his chin bleeding profusely. Annie gasped as he grabbed her arm and half-dragged her over to Luke and Jeremiah. Terrified, Annie thought Jeremiah was dead, and that Luke would be next.

Luke jumped up and made for Weatherford as though to kill him, but two soldiers headed him off, ramming their muskets into his gut.

"Let go of my wife!" Luke roared.

Weatherford shoved Annie aside so hard that she nearly fell. "You lied to me! You knew your brother was here. I should arrest you right along *with* him!"

"No!" Annie screamed.

Weatherford grabbed a handkerchief from a pocket inside his coat and held it to his chin. "Shut the wench up!" he ordered Luke.

Luke pulled her protectively close. "We have to help Jeremiah!" he demanded. "He's still alive!"

Weatherford glowered at him, holding the blood-saturated handkerchief to his chin. "It is only because of orders from the king himself that I don't this moment give orders to put a bullet in your brother's head and finish him off! Now we'll have to stay in this damned excuse for a settlement until he is healed enough to travel back with us. Where is the closest place to take him?"

"My father's house!" Annie quickly answered. She looked up at Luke. "It's right here in town, and it's the only logical place to take Jeremiah now. He'll bleed to death if we don't do something quickly!"

Luke glared at Weatherford. "If my brother dies—"

"He shot at me first," Weatherford reminded him.

"After you put your sword to my wife and then ran me down, you bloody coward!"

Weatherford stiffened visibly. "You are damnably close to going to prison right along with your brother," he told Luke through gritted teeth. "But since he is your brother, and since I understand your frustration over this, it being your wedding day—" he looked Annie over scathingly "—I will let your insults go. But you had better curb your tongue, Mr. Wilde, or it will be a long time before you share a bed with your new wife!"

Weatherford turned and ordered his men to help get Jeremiah to the Barnes home. Luke quickly procured a flatbed wagon from one of the visiting colonists and asked the soldiers to load Jeremiah onto it. Annie noticed rage in her father's eyes. Surely he'd not thought he might see his daughter and her husband abused or arrested on what was just minutes earlier a wonderful, happy day for him. She also saw a terrible anger on both her brothers' faces, and she knew that this one incident had changed a lot of things for many of the people in Willow Creek. Many who had proclaimed themselves neutral toward the revolution would change their minds.

Weatherford cursed Jeremiah as one of his men tended to his own wound. "Damned murdering bastard meant to put a lead ball through my head!" he lamented. "If I hadn't moved just when he got off that shot . . . He'll damn well pay for this!"

Yes, he surely will, Annie thought. They would take Jeremiah away! He would hang! And he would suffer through it all alone, with not even the woman he loved at his side. She felt a heavy weight on her heart as the wagon carrying Jeremiah creaked and clattered away toward her father's house.

Luke put an arm around her. "Let's go," he said, starting to walk behind the wagon.

"Luke, please don't give that Englishman any more trouble," she begged. "You'll get yourself arrested. What would I do if they took you away, too?"

"Let's just take one thing at a time. Right now, we have to help Jeremiah."

Several others followed them, and soldiers rode beside them, behind them, swords drawn. Weatherford, gauze wrapped from under his chin around his head, rode to catch up, prancing his horse beside the wagon. He looked so angry and arrogant. Annie knew he was waiting for just one more excuse to beat or arrest Luke.

They reached the Barnes home, and men quickly carried Jeremiah inside. Annie's mother had hurried ahead, and by the time Annie got inside, Jeremiah was laid out on the kitchen table.

Ethel Barnes was giving quiet orders to the men standing nearby.
Luke hurried over and stripped off Jeremiah's shirt and vest,
while Ethel poured hot water into a bowl and washed off her
kitchen knife.

"Let me help," Annie offered.

"This is your wedding day," Luke answered. "Just—" He
turned to face her, terrible regret and sorrow in his eyes. "Go
change your dress so you don't get blood on it." He touched her
face. "I never even got the chance to tell you how beautiful you
look today, Annie. I'm so sorry for all of this. Jeremiah is my
brother, and if he hadn't come here—"

"It's all right, Luke. It's not his fault. It's the fault of the
English, and the war and—"

"No, it's not all right," he interrupted. "This was supposed
to be our night. Now . . ." He closed his eyes. "Damn all of this!"
He ran a thumb over her cheek. "Go change, Annie. We'll talk
later."

He turned back to Jeremiah, and Annie walked over to climb
into the loft where she'd slept most of her life. Tonight she was
supposed to have slept in her new home . . . Luke's home. Tonight she was supposed to lie in Luke's arms and become his
wife in every way.

She looked down from the loft at a half-naked Jeremiah
lying on the table, her mother giving orders, Luke standing over
Jeremiah with a knife and telling Annie's brothers and two other
men to hold Jeremiah's legs and arms. Annie's father poured
whiskey down Jeremiah's throat, and Annie could not help the
tears that streamed down her face when Jeremiah cried out in
pain as Luke began cutting into him. At the same time, the
delicious aroma of deer meat roasting behind her family's home
wafted through the windows—the deer that had been hunted
and killed by Jeremiah for the wedding feast, just as he'd prom-

ised. Now English soldiers would likely help themselves to the succulent meat.

Annie looked away from the blood that poured from Jeremiah's side. Her wedding day had turned into the worst day of her life.

7

Annie came down from the loft wearing a simple brown homespun dress and an apron, ready to help in any way she could. Luke was finished, and Jeremiah lay still as death, his face an ashen color. Ethel was packing the wound with moss, and she asked Annie to help her wrap it.

After washing blood from his hands, Luke sat in a chair near Jeremiah, his elbows on his knees and his hands over his face. Annie's father and brothers sat nearby, all of the men somber. Sally left to fetch more water, and Annie tore strips of cloth from a bolt of material to make bandages that would hold the moss tightly at the wound. No one knew why, but moss seemed to help draw the poison out of wounds to stave off infection.

Annie struggled to keep her hands from shaking as she helped wrap the wound. Luke got up to help lift Jeremiah enough that they could keep passing the cloth underneath him, and again Annie felt the guilt of knowing she'd lain with Jeremiah; yet this was the first time she'd seen fully his bare torso. Their night of passion had brought their bodies together in a way that taught her the mystery of man, yet she'd never actually looked upon that part of him now covered with a blanket. He'd taken her by the dim light of a lantern in the barn loft, getting under her skirt but not undressing her.

Now here he was possibly dying on the family dining table, and she was his brother's wife. It all seemed so incredibly unreal. She heard shouted orders outside to watch every window and door of the house and make sure Jeremiah did not escape. Apparently, Jeremiah was an even more able man than she'd thought. How foolish it was to think he could escape in his condition. Even if he was awake right now, he likely would not even be able to sit up.

"I'm sorry to bring you all this trouble," Luke told Ethel.

"It's not your doing," she answered. "Things happen. I'm more sorry for you and Annie."

Annie looked up at Luke, who gazed at her longingly. "I'm so sorry, Annie. This sure isn't the way we were supposed to spend the day . . . and night."

Annie felt the blood rush to her cheeks as her mother heard the comment.

"The two of you should go on ahead to your place," Ethel told Luke. "You should be alone tonight."

"No," Luke answered. "I'll not leave here until Jeremiah does. Besides, I'm not leaving your family alone with those damn soldiers breathing down your necks. I'll stay until it's determined what will happen to Jeremiah. And if he gets even worse, I should be here. Besides, after all of this, Annie and I couldn't . . . it just . . . I just don't want it to be like this. There will be a better time."

"I understand." Ethel tied off the cloth strip, and Luke reached out to touch Annie's arm.

"Do *you* understand, Annie?"

She put a hand over his. "Of course I do."

"Okay, boys, let's move Jeremiah into Jake's bed." The words came from Annie's father.

Jake, Luke, Calvin, and Henry lifted Jeremiah as gently as possible and carried him into the room where Annie's brothers slept. Jeremiah groaned but did not seem to actually wake up. Annie helped her mother wash blood from the table, feeling sick at Jeremiah's condition. Once he was settled in, all the men returned to the main room. Annie's father sat down wearily and lit his pipe.

"What the hell do we do now?" he asked Luke before drawing several times on the pipe to heat the tobacco in its bowl. Annie thought he looked very tired.

"I wish I knew," Luke answered.

"I say we all go East and fight with the Patriots against the damned English!" Jake grumbled.

"Keep your voice down!" his father ordered in a near whisper. "Don't be talking traitorous talk with those soldiers right outside the door."

"Yes, we need to be careful," Luke told Jake. "Weatherford is itching to find a reason to arrest all of us."

"But what about Jeremiah?" Calvin asked. "You gonna' let them take him away, Luke?"

"I don't know. I have to think. I can't do something that will risk the lives and property of Willow Creek. And I certainly can't do something that could make my wife a widow before we've even had a chance to have a life together."

"I say we help Jeremiah find a way to escape again once he's well enough," Henry said, staring at the floor as he puffed on his pipe. "There has to be a way to do that without it looking like our fault. He's a clever man. Once he's free of them, he'll find a way to stay free until this damned war is over. He must have friends back East who would hide him. Hell, he's friends with that so-called President, George Washington, on account of your pa."

"That's true," Luke said. "The problem is finding a way to get Jeremiah out of this mess first. The Patriots are gaining ground and refuse to give up, and from some of the things Jeremiah told me that the English have been doing to the colonists, and after what we saw today, I'm beginning to see their point. We're just so far removed out here from what's going on, and we're so involved with worrying about Indian attacks, that we haven't been paying enough attention to this whole mess. Now the war has come to us, too."

Annie washed her hands in a clean bowl of water and dried them on her apron. "Luke, you aren't thinking of joining the Patriot cause, are you? You won't go off like Jeremiah did and not come back?"

He glanced up at her from where he sat, then leaned back and ran both hands through his hair. "No...I don't think so. But I can help by at least finding a way to help Jeremiah get away."

"But if they catch you, they'll hang you, too!" She walked closer, the horror of the possibility of both brothers hanging sending waves of panic through her blood.

Luke motioned for her to sit down on his lap. She did so, relishing the feel of his strong arms around her as she laid her head on his shoulder.

"No one is going to hang," he told her. "Not me...and not Jeremiah. I'll make sure of it."

8

July 26, 1780

Per her mother's instructions, Annie took a bowl of hot chicken broth to Jeremiah, who lay against a pile of feather pillows. For three days, the broth and a little bread were all he'd been able to eat, and that after the first two days of lying near unconsciousness and eating nothing. Luke had tended to his brother faithfully, helped by Annie's father or one of her brothers when Jeremiah needed to be turned over or lifted. Her mother had kept the dressings of his wound changed, and so far, in spite of signs of redness and swelling around the wound itself, no infection had appeared. A slight fever had disappeared, a good sign that Jeremiah would heal.

Now it was Annie's turn to help with feeding him. She'd not had a chance to speak with him alone since the shooting. Today life had returned to as normal as could be expected, what with soldiers milling about outside and Colonel Weatherford constantly barging in to see how well Jeremiah was doing. The man was anxious to drag Jeremiah off to New York, and Annie feared he would do just that before Jeremiah was ready to travel.

Jeremiah lay awake watching her as she came into the room.

His muscled arms, chest, and shoulders were bare, the blankets pulled up just past the wrappings on his wound.

"It's my turn to feed you," Annie told him, taking a chair beside the bed.

He closed his eyes for a moment and sighed, shifting slightly and wincing with pain as he did so. "I'm sorry," he said softly, "for this mess."

"It's the fault of that Colonel Weatherford."

He looked at her again. "We all know it's my fault . . . for coming back here in the first place. I've not only ruined your wedding day, but I've put this whole village in danger, especially Luke and you and your family."

"What's done is done," Annie answered, dipping a spoon into the broth. "What you need to do now is eat and get your strength back."

"So Weatherford can watch me hang?"

Annie felt sick. "Please don't say that. You're supposed to get a fair trial."

He closed his eyes again. "It won't be fair, I assure you."

"Surely if you tell them at your trial the things they did to you and the other men on that ship—"

He waved her off. "The English like hanging people they consider traitors. They figure sights like that will teach the colonists a lesson."

His voice was weak, and his words came haltingly from the pain. Annie couldn't help hurting for him. "What will you do, Jeremiah? It's all so unfair!"

He reached out for her. "Set that bowl aside," he said weakly.

Annie set the broth on a night table and took his hand, noticing how dark his skin was next to hers. He squeezed her hand with what strength he had. "I don't want you to worry about it. I already have a plan."

She frowned. "What plan?"

"It's best you don't know anything about it." He looked toward the doorway. "Where is Luke?"

"The soldiers let him go back to his place to tend to his livestock and check his fields. He'll be back tonight."

"You should have gone with him, Annie. The two of you haven't even had a chance to be husband and wife."

Annie felt embarrassed and pulled her hand away. "The right time will come. It can't be when we're both worried about what will happen to you."

"I told you I have that little problem solved. Luke just needs to get back here before Weatherford decides to haul me away."

"Luke! Don't tell me he's part of your plan. He could be killed!"

He managed a soft smile as he looked her over lovingly. "You have to trust me, Annie. I know what I'm doing. Luke is helping in a way that means he won't be involved with those damn soldiers out there."

"How can he *not* be involved?"

"He'll be all right, Annie." He closed his eyes from weariness. "I promise."

Annie sighed with exasperation. "You're always so sure of yourself, aren't you? Don't forget you're playing with my husband's life."

He shifted in bed and grimaced with pain. "Annie, Annie, Annie. He's my *brother*." He grasped her hand again. "*Trust* me. Look me in the eyes and tell me you trust me."

Wanting to cry for fear of the danger both men were in, she obeyed his request. He squeezed her hand again reassuringly.

"Luke will be all right."

Annie pursed her lips in thought. "You haven't exactly given me reason to trust you, Jeremiah. You ran out on me, and now you're back, bringing all this trouble with you—"

"Annie, how many ways are there to say I'm sorry? I only know of one, and I've said it. And I never thought those damn soldiers would come clear out here looking for me."

"Well, it only shows the kind of trouble you can get yourself into, doesn't it? Now you're getting Luke involved."

"In a safe way, I assure you. I love you, Annie. And naturally, I love my brother. I don't want anything to happen to him any more than you do. Surely you know that. I wish I could tell you more, but it's best that I don't."

She managed a smile through tears, shaking her head. "You sure have a strange way of showing people that you love them."

He smiled in return, massaging her hand gently. "I guess I do." He sighed. "Look, Annie, once I'm gone—"

Suddenly someone pounded on the outer door. "Open up, Mrs. Barnes! It's Colonel Weatherford!"

Annie pulled her hand away and jumped up, wondering how Weatherford could possibly think they wouldn't recognize his voice by now. She'd grown to hate the sound of it. She stood beside the bed while her mother opened the door.

"Why don't you leave us alone?" Ethel asked.

"I want to know Jeremiah's condition. It's time we got underway. I'm sick of this place!"

"He's far too sick to travel for several more days yet," Ethel answered.

"I'll be the judge of that!" Weatherford stormed into the room where Jeremiah lay and glared at him. "So, it appears you will live."

"Sorry to disappoint you," Jeremiah answered weakly.

Weatherford turned to Annie, and she took pleasure in the sight of the large, ugly scab on the man's chin.

"You had better hope your husband and family are not up

to some plan to try to help this man escape," Weatherford threatened. "Or you will be a widow before you've even been fully a wife!" He looked back at Jeremiah. "Two days. That's all you have. In two days, we leave for New York!" He turned and walked out, his heavy boots pounding against the plank floor.

The outer door closed with a slam, and Annie faced Jeremiah, her heart racing with dread. "Two days aren't enough! A trip like that will *kill* you, Jeremiah!"

A look of such deep hatred came into his eyes that it actually frightened her. "Well, I'm sure that's his plan, but I have a plan of my own. We'll see who ends up dying."

Annie's stomach tightened at the comment. Whatever Jeremiah had in mind, Luke was also involved. She could only pray that Weatherford was not right about her becoming a widow before she'd even truly been a wife.

9

Just as Colonel Weatherford promised, he came for Jeremiah, his soldiers filling the small family cabin, threatening Luke and Annie's father and brothers with bayonets while men went into the room where Jeremiah lay and ordered him to get dressed.

"He can hardly stand up yet!" Luke argued. "How do you expect him to dress himself?"

"We can always drag him out naked if he prefers," Weatherford answered sarcastically.

They all heard a groan from the curtained room. "For God's sake, let me go help him!" Luke begged.

Weatherford frowned at one of his men. "Keep a close watch on him," he ordered.

Luke stormed into the bedroom, and Annie felt a rage deep in her soul. "So," she sneered, "it takes three armed soldiers to watch just two men, one of them so sick he can't even stand? You must not have much confidence in your men, Colonel Weatherford."

The man stepped closer to her, his dark eyes narrowing as he rested the end of his bayonet on her shoulder. "And you are lucky that I am leaving your beloved husband behind, Mrs. Wilde," he answered. "Watch your tongue, or you'll be watching me drag *him* away, too!"

"For doing nothing more than helping his own brother? I daresay you would do the same, unless you are even more heartless than you appear. Do you have a brother, Colonel?"

He reddened slightly, pursing his lips as he stepped back. "My brothers have sense enough not to betray the king."

"Perhaps if the king—"

"Annie!" her father interrupted. "Don't make a bad situation worse!"

Annie did not finish, but she continued glaring at the colonel.

"Your father is a wise man," Weatherford told her. He moved away from her and barked at the men in the room with Jeremiah. "Hurry up in there!"

Annie wanted to cry when she heard another groan from Jeremiah. He could die on the way back to New York and they wouldn't even know it. Her only prayer was that he could escape on the way, as he'd claimed he would, but how was that possible, what with the condition he was in?

Finally, Jeremiah came out of the room, wearing his buckskins, much more comfortable and looser clothing than the shirt and pants he'd been wearing when he was shot. She realized the looser clothing was better suited for not aggravating his wound. In spite of his dark skin, he looked gray. His uncombed hair was pulled back and tied, and it took Luke and one of the soldiers to help him stand.

"Look at him!" she pleaded to Weatherford, wanting to cry. "He'll die on the way if you don't let him have a few more days to heal!"

"Well then, that will save us the nuisance of a trial, won't it?"

"You bastard!" Luke growled.

Weatherford stepped close to him and ordered him to step away from his brother. "One of my men will take over now," he told Luke.

Reluctantly, Luke let go of Jeremiah, who stood glaring at Weatherford in spite of his weakened condition. Annie knew he was in a great deal of pain but refused to let Weatherford see how much he was suffering. That would only please the man.

One of the other soldiers took Luke's place and helped Jeremiah walk out. Before leaving, Weatherford suddenly turned and, without warning, whacked the butt of his long gun across the side of Luke's face.

Annie screamed as Luke crumpled. "Luke!" She ran to his side as Weatherford walked out. Young Calvin started for the door, fists clenched, but his father grabbed him and stopped him.

"Let it go for now, Calvin!"

"The dirty bastard!" Calvin exclaimed.

The right side of Luke's face bled profusely from a deep cut. Annie held his arm as he got to his knees and groaned. "Oh, Luke, my God!"

"Let me go!" he said, getting to his feet.

"Luke, don't go out there! They'd love an excuse to beat you more, or even to shoot you!" Annie pleaded.

Luke put a hand to his face. "I wonder how that sonofabitch would like to face me in a fair fight," he sneered. Blood streamed through his fingers and down his shirtsleeve. He headed for the door.

"Luke!" Annie screamed. "Don't go!"

He hesitated at the door, then stumbled to a chair, looking ready to pass out. "Go see him off," he asked Annie and the others. "Let him know we'll all pray for him."

One by one, they stepped outside. Jeremiah was laid out in

a wagon Weatherford had confiscated from one of the settlers. Annie thought how horribly painful it would be for him, bouncing around in that wagon.

"After a few days, he'll walk the rest of the way," Weatherford said, facing the family. Many from the settlement stood about watching, some shouting curses at the soldiers. Annie knew that already a few secret meetings had been held where people talked about what they should do, and many who were once uninvolved now talked about joining the Patriots, even though this war had been going on for four years and there still was not a real victor. It seemed incredible that the colonists could ever win out over a government and army as mighty as England's, but Annie finally could see why they were trying.

"Say your last good-byes," Weatherford told them.

Each family member took a turn leaning over the wagon to touch Jeremiah's shoulder and tell him they would pray for him. Henry Barnes held up a crying twelve-year-old Sally, who was very short for her age, so that she could tell Jeremiah she hoped he would be all right. The young girl shook with sobs, horrified at the violence she'd seen over the last several days. "They hurt Luke," she wept.

Annie was next. She stood on a slight lip at the bed of the wagon so she could lean closer. "God go with you, Jeremiah," she said softly, wiping at tears that came too fast to keep up with.

He managed to take her hand. "What did they do to Luke?"

"Weatherford hit him across the face with his gun. He's pretty dazed."

Jeremiah closed his eyes with anger. "I'll kill him," he said in quiet rage.

There was a determined coldness to the words that told Annie he would try to do just that, given the chance. She sensed there was a ruthlessness to Jeremiah she'd never seen, and probably did not care to see.

"I don't know what to say, Jeremiah," she wept. "You know how I feel. All I can say now is good-bye. I'll pray for you always and forever."

He managed a faint smile. "That's good enough for me," he told her. "Be good to Luke, and don't be afraid, Annie, no matter what happens. Don't doubt anything Luke does, and don't try to stop him. I'll make sure nothing happens to him, like I promised."

There was no chance to say any more. Weatherford ordered his men to get underway, and the wagon jerked as the soldier at the reins snapped a whip to get the horses moving. Annie had to jump down quickly, and the wagon clattered away. The weather had been extremely dry, and dust rolled from beneath the wagon wheels, becoming even thicker as thirty or so soldiers followed on horseback.

Weatherford put his horse into a faster trot so he could move to the front of the column, and the crowd stood in silent rage as wagon and soldiers gradually rounded a bend in the road and disappeared into the surrounding woods. Annie felt as though something had gripped her stomach and twisted it. She wiped at her tears and went back inside to find her mother holding a wet cloth to Luke's face. When she took it away, Annie could see a purple swelling on his right cheekbone.

"Luke!" She hurried to take over for her mother. She rinsed the bloodied cloth and wrung it out, again pressing it to the wound.

Luke put a hand over hers. "They're gone?"

"Yes," she answered, leaning up and kissing his other cheek. "Are you going to be all right?"

"I have to be. There is something I have to do," he told her, an anger in his eyes she'd never seen before. She felt numb with fear.

"Luke, don't tell me—"

"I have to do it, Annie."

"But if you help Jeremiah, you'll be arrested, too!"

"Not necessarily."

"Luke, what do you mean? Jeremiah can't even walk on his own!"

"He won't have to, although if he could, everything would be a lot easier. Jeremiah can be as fierce and wild as a mother bear just coming out of a cave in the spring. Weatherford should be damned glad he's *not* at full strength, believe me."

"But then how can you help Jeremiah if he can't—"

"Don't ask questions, Annie." He closed his eyes for a moment, then met her gaze. "Saddle my horse," he told her.

"Luke!"

"Just do what I ask, Annie. Your mother can fix up needle and thread and sew my cheek shut while you do that."

"You don't even have any weapons!" she reminded him. "They're at the farm."

He put a finger to her lips. "Saddle my horse," he said again, softly but sternly. "Just trust me, Annie, and trust Jeremiah. He's lived in the wilds, and he's befriended the right people in the right places."

Their gazes held as Annie tried to decipher what he was telling her. *"Indians?"* she asked in a whisper.

Luke frowned. "We're wasting time."

"Luke, half the Indians around would just as soon scalp and torture you as not," she reminded him in a soft but angry voice.

He put a hand over her mouth. "Do as I say, Annie. And be sure to tell everyone that I'm going to the farm to make sure

Weatherford doesn't try to stop there and destroy it."

Annie wanted to scream. Luke would be putting himself in terrible danger, over a plan that might not work at all. If it failed, he could either be murdered by Indians or shot by the soldiers or, at best, arrested. Yet he and Jeremiah were asking her to *trust* them?

Feeling removed from reality, she turned away and walked to the door, then stopped. "Luke is going to check on the farm. He's worried that Weatherford will stop there," she told her mother. "You'll need to sew up his cheek while I saddle his horse."

"Of course," Ethel answered, already threading a needle.

Annie felt sick at the thought of the pain the stitches would bring Luke. She wished this whole nightmare would end. As she walked out to the barn, she noticed bones left from the deer carcass roasted for her wedding feast lay scattered on the ground, totally cleaned off and partially chewed by dogs.

The wedding. It hardly seemed real anymore. She looked down at the gold band on her finger. She and Luke had been married for seven days, and still the marriage had not been consummated.

Maybe it never would be.

10

August 5, 1780

Annie threw dried corn to the chickens. She'd finished milking
Luke's two cows, and fresh bread dough sat rising in the kitchen.
It wasn't until after Luke left and she'd come here to wait for
him that she'd discovered his wedding present to her. In the
kitchen area sat a beautiful oak, handmade china cabinet, filled
with china shipped all the way from New England. According
to her father, it was meant to be a surprise when Luke brought
her home on their wedding night.

Annie wondered if they would ever be able to share their
new home together. Luke had been gone a week. Her stomach
cramped at the thought of all the possibilities: arrested, horribly
injured, maybe murdered and scalped by Indians. What if Luke
and Jeremiah were both dead? She'd heard nothing since the day
Jeremiah was taken away and Luke rode out after him.

Was she already the widow of a man she'd never even shared
a bed with? She turned to watch her father chopping wood, and
again she noticed that some of the vigor was gone out of him.
What was once an easy chore was now difficult for him, and she
suspected much of his lassitude was due to his worry and anger

over events since her wedding day. His musket was propped nearby, primed and ready to shoot . . . just in case.

Annie loved him for coming to stay with her here, and she realized he was just as concerned about Luke as she was. Henry, too, had hoped the war would not come to Willow Creek. The fighting had been raging back East for nearly four years, and most thought it might be over by this time. Now all the talk was about Patriots and Continentals, Tories and Loyalists. Annie could not imagine how, even if America won independence, there could ever be a truly organized government or any real peace again.

She tipped the grain basket upside down and shook out the last of the corn, then headed back toward the house, stopping to pet Luke's dog, Lucifer. The black, shaggy mongrel was as wild as it was tame, and had been missing during the barn raising, returning only a few days ago. Annie hoped the dog's return was a good sign, but that hope was dwindling.

Lucifer left her and began chasing chickens, and Annie shouted at the animal to leave the poor creatures alone. Just as she did so, Lucifer suddenly whirled and began barking wildly, charging down the narrow dirt roadway that led to the farm. It was then that Annie noticed him, a lone rider approaching. Her first thought was that the visitor might be one of her brothers, or that perhaps someone from town was bringing a message.

"Pa?" she shouted. She set down the basket and walked partway down the path. The figure came closer, and now she recognized Luke's large gray gelding with its unusual, almost perfect triangular-shaped white spot on its chest. "Luke," she murmured. She began running toward him, and already Lucifer was leaping at horse and man. Annie waited, alarmed at the pain in Luke's eyes.

The horse reached her, and she touched Luke's leg. "Luke, what happened? Are you hurt?"

He appeared confused, his gaze seeming to go through her rather than actually seeing her.

"Luke? Talk to me! Is Jeremiah all right? Did he get away? Are the soldiers gone?"

"I think Jeremiah will be all right," he answered.

"What about you? My God, Luke, you're covered with blood! Your shirt! Your pants—"

"I'm all right." He slowly dismounted, ordering Lucifer to quiet down. The panting dog let out a whine of excitement, then paced in circles around them as Luke half-leaned against his horse, his entire countenance seeming weary. He sighed deeply. "We have to . . . burn these clothes. And if anyone comes asking, I've been right here with you all week. We're newlyweds, so why would they doubt that?"

"Of course, Luke. That was the whole plan." Annie grasped his arms. "Luke, thank God you're all right!"

Luke put an arm around her and led her toward the house as her father came to greet them.

"Luke, son, what happened? You look terrible! Are you wounded?"

"No. I'm just . . . tired. I've been riding two days straight. I need you to take care of my horse for me."

"Of course. It sure is a relief to see you." Henry looked past him down the pathway. "No one's after you?"

Luke shook his head, stopping then and looking from Henry to Annie and again to Henry. "There is no one *left* to come after me."

Annie gasped, putting a hand to her mouth. "All those English soldiers?"

Luke looked away. "They're all dead. Some worse than dead."

"Even Colonel Weatherford?" Henry asked.

Luke nodded. "Yeah, even the colonel. I've never seen anything like it. I'm sure Jeremiah has, but not me. Believe it or not, I actually felt sorry for the man."

"What happened?" Annie asked.

"What about Jeremiah?" Henry asked before Luke could answer.

"I can't talk about it now," Luke told them. "Jeremiah is with friends," he told Henry.

"Indians?" Annie asked.

Luke nodded. "Right now I just want to wash up, and I need to burn these clothes." He handed his horse's reins to Henry. "Brush him down good and turn him out. For safety's sake, I don't want someone coming around to see my horse the mess he is."

It was then that Annie realized even Luke's horse had blood on him, besides being filthy and lathered.

Henry put a wrinkled, weathered hand on Luke's shoulder. "I'll take care of your horse, son. You go on in and get cleaned up. And Lord knows, you and Annie deserve some time alone. There will be a better time to explain all that happened. I'll tend your horse and finish some chores, and I'll sleep in the barn tonight . . . head home in the morning. You come see us and tell us everything soon as you're ready."

"Thanks, Henry. I appreciate everything you've done to help out."

"You're family now, Luke. You and your brother always did seem like family, even before you decided to marry Annie." Henry took Luke's horse and headed toward the barn.

Luke turned to his wife. "I'm sorry for what you've had to go through, all the waiting and wondering."

"Luke, you've come back alive and unhurt," Annie said. "That's all that matters right now. Come inside."

He walked with her to the house, stopping before going up the porch steps. "I imagined you sitting on this porch rocking our babies," he told her.

She grasped his hand. "And I will be, Luke."

He looked at her with an odd sorrow that made her want to cry. "I hope so."

Annie helped him inside, and Luke went into their downstairs bedroom to undress. Annie hurriedly took a kettle of hot water from the fireplace and poured some of the water into a washbowl, then mixed cooler water into it. She carried the bowl to the washstand in the bedroom, where Luke was already stripping off his clothes and throwing them on the floor.

Annie could not help noticing his powerful build, feeling flustered at seeing him naked from the waist up for the first time. She looked away when he met her gaze.

"Burn these," he told her.

She turned to pick up his woolen pants and the shirt he'd worn, still somewhat stunned at how much blood stained his clothes. As she rose from picking up the garments, he was stripping off his long johns, as though he'd undressed in front of her before.

"Add those to the fire," he told her.

Annie averted her gaze, feeling a sudden apprehension at the realization that she was his wife now, which meant he could do with her as he pleased. She was not prepared for the odd change in his demeanor, a rather commanding attitude she'd never seen in him before.

She walked out with the clothes, taking them to her father and asking him to start a brush fire and burn them for her.

"He okay?" Henry asked.

"I think so. He's so . . . I don't know . . . different, Pa."

"War and killing will do that to a man, Annie." He patted her shoulder. "Just let him do the talking. He'll get back to his old self soon enough."

Annie walked back to the house, taking her time so Luke would be able to wash and get dressed. When she arrived, he was still in the curtained-off bedroom. "Do you want some tea?" she asked him.

He came through the curtain wearing his pants, but no socks or shirt. "Make yourself some tea if you want," he told her, going to the other end of the room to take a pouch of tobacco from his smoking table. He filled his pipe. "I'll have a shot of whiskey."

Annie frowned but asked no questions. She scooped shredded tea leaves from a canister and packed them into a strainer, which she then put into a heavy ceramic cup. She poured hot water into the cup, then walked to the cupboard where Luke kept a flask of whiskey, meant more for treating wounds than for drinking. Luke came over to the table with a lit pipe, sitting down and puffing on it while Annie handed him the whiskey and a small glass.

"Thanks." Luke poured what looked to Annie like more than just a shot of the wicked drink. He downed it in one gulp, then just sat there for a few seconds with his head tipped back and his eyes closed before letting out a long sigh.

Annie sat down across from him, dipping her tea strainer up and down in the cup and waiting for Luke to talk.

"Everything all right here?" he finally asked.

"Yes, but Luke, the more important question is . . . is everything all right with you?"

He leaned forward, elbows on the table. "It will be." He drew on his pipe again before pouring another drink. He glanced at her as he set the flask aside. "Don't worry. I won't get drunk and beat you or anything."

Annie frowned. "Beat me?"

He finally smiled a little, although a terrible sadness still shone in his blue eyes. "I was kidding, Annie. I just meant . . . I know I don't seem in a very good mood, and you've never seen me drink before. Considering the fact that this will be our first night together since we got married, I expect you're not crazy about seeing me imbibing."

Annie felt her cheeks warming. "I know something terrible happened, Luke, and I know men sometimes turn to drink over certain things." She reached out and touched his arm. "You can talk to me, you know. I'm your wife. I want to know what happened." She studied his handsome face, still finding it hard to believe he was really here in the flesh and unhurt. "You look so weary."

He lowered the pipe. "It was a nightmare," he answered. "I've been forced to kill a couple of Indians over the last few years, but this was . . . different. This time, the Indians weren't the enemy." He leaned back, drawing on his pipe again for a few quiet seconds.

Annie sipped some of the tea, thinking it still was not steeped enough.

"Jeremiah told me where to find a Delaware man who called himself Jimmy Bear. He and Jeremiah used to hunt together, and Jimmy Bear knew the right warriors—Iroquois who enjoy making war and enjoy killing Redcoats. It took me two days to find the man, and he and his cohorts were more than willing to stage an Indian attack to help Jeremiah escape. I thought that's all that would happen, but as we know from stories we've heard about other Indian attacks on our own people, the Iroquois never do anything in a small way." He rubbed at his eyes. "We've heard a lot of horror stories about how the Iroquois can torture, how they will sometimes carve the heart out of a live man and eat it while it's still beating."

Annie winced. "They didn't—"

"No. But the slaughter that took place made me feel sick. I didn't plan on all the soldiers dying like that, not even Weatherford, much as he deserved it. He did not die quickly." He smoked quietly for a moment. "Then again, we didn't dare let even one Englishman get away. It had to look like it was strictly an unplanned Indian attack, so that none of us will be suspected of being a part of it. Even the folks in town think I've been here. It happened near another settlement quite a bit farther upriver. Those people will find the bodies, or what's left of them, and it will be reported as an Indian attack. There will be no doubt of that, by what they will find . . . bodies stripped near naked, body parts cut off, most of them scalped, weapons and horses taken." He closed his eyes and shook his head.

"Jeremiah?" Annie asked.

A hint of a smile passed his lips. "Sick as he was, he managed to climb out of the wagon and take a knife off a dead Indian. He stabbed one soldier in the back, another in the heart, before collapsing. I didn't know he could be that vicious, but then, he can be as Indian as they come. I'd hate to see what he could do when he's healthy. Jimmy Bear and two of his friends got him on a horse then and took him off someplace while the rest of them . . . finished their job. I haven't seen Jeremiah since."

He puffed on the pipe again, staring at the wood floor. "I guess killing comes easy to Jeremiah now. A man does enough of it, he learns not to let it bother him. I was watching from behind some pine trees because Jeremiah ordered me to stay out of sight in case one of the soldiers got away. He wanted to make sure I couldn't be accused of helping him escape. Still, a couple of soldiers got around behind me somehow and came at me. I turned and fired my musket, getting one right in his belly. The other one came at me with his bayonet. I swung my musket and got him across the side of the head. I managed to move aside just enough so that he missed me. He went down, and I . . . I don't know. A man just does what he has to do to protect himself and his own, I guess. I grabbed the soldier's musket and plunged the bayonet into his heart. Blood just . . . it just . . . kind of flew out of him . . . and all over me. The next minute, the Iroquois were on him, robbing him of every piece of clothing as well as his scalp."

He shook his head again. "It's all so crazy, Annie. I mean, I've shot Indians from a distance, but I've never killed up close like that. A week ago, I was happy to be getting married, and I had little interest in this war. Now English blood is on my hands. I feel like I'm as involved as if I was part of the Continental Army, which is probably where Jeremiah will end up once he's healed. I'm sure his friend Jimmy Bear will take good care of him, with the help of some very willing Indian maidens, no doubt."

Annie's relief at knowing Jeremiah would be all right was tainted by the thought of him enjoying the pleasures of some young Indian woman, maybe more than one. Still, what could she expect? He was a man, and probably very lonely right now. If an Indian woman could relieve that loneliness, she was glad. "When you talked before all of this, did he say where he would go once he was healed?"

Luke shrugged. "Probably to find George Washington. He'll help Jeremiah any way he can. And you know Jeremiah. He finds ways to survive. He always has and always will, just like in this latest mess." He straightened and looked at her. "I'm part of it now, Annie. I'm not sure I can just let it end here."

Now alarm engulfed her. "What do you mean? Please don't go off and join the Patriots, Luke! You promised you wouldn't."

He studied her lovingly, some of the horror leaving his eyes. "And I will keep my promise, as much as fate will allow me to keep it. But I've seen a side to the English I never saw before, and I don't like it. I've listened to Jeremiah, and he makes sense. It's people like us, Annie, who have made this country what it is. It's us who've fought Indians and suffered horribly for it. It's us who've put blood and sweat into opening up this land, but it's England who profits from it and tells us how to live, where we can sell our goods, how much taxes we'll have to pay. We have no say in those things. Hell, the king has never even been to America. And men like George Washington, well-educated men, men of money and influence, they're willing to risk everything they own as well as their very lives to change all that. They are fighting for *us,* Annie, and everybody like us, so we can be free of tyranny and free to set our own laws and rules, free to trade with whomever we want to trade. It makes me feel guilty . . . like I'm not doing enough."

"You came home covered with an Englishman's blood, Luke! You helped your brother escape so *he* could go and fight. Jeremiah would want you to come right back here and keep farming and . . ." *and take care of me,* she wanted to add. She looked down at her cup of tea. "Not every man can leave home and responsibilities to fight this war, Luke. While we're fighting, people and the army have to eat. Someone has to do the farming and provide what's needed. There are more parts to play in a war than just shooting and killing. Maybe your responsibility is to stay right here and keep doing what you're doing."

He sighed deeply again. "I guess you're right." He set his

pipe aside and stood up to walk around to where she sat. "I have a lot to think about, Annie. And if you don't mind, I've got to sleep for a while. I'm so damned tired I can't think straight."

"You should eat something first."

"I ate some jerked meat. Besides, I don't have an appetite yet."

Annie rose and faced him. "Then that's what you should do. I've got bread ready to be baked, and stew simmering over the fire." She raised her gaze to meet his, feeling embarrassingly brazen standing with her face so close to his bare chest. "Maybe if you sleep a while, you'll be ready to eat when you wake up."

Their eyes held in unspoken thoughts. Maybe he would be ready for more than that. She was his wife now. A few days ago, they had been so ready to make that a reality, before the *un*reality of what took place after that.

Luke nodded. "Maybe," he answered. He leaned down and kissed her forehead. "I love you, Annie."

"And I love you."

He touched her face, then walked around the table and into the bedroom. Annie watched after him, feeling terror at the thought that he might decide to run off and join the war.

11

August 6, 1780

"He's still sleeping." Annie spooned more stew into a bowl for her father's second helping. It was past noon, and Annie had given up waiting for Luke to wake up and join them for lunch.

"That's good. It's what he needs."

Annie hung the stew kettle back on a spit over the hearth. "It's been nearly sixteen hours. I've never seen someone sleep so hard for so long. I keep going in and touching him to make sure he's still alive." She sat down to yet another cup of tea. The bread was baked, and she'd pressed her butter into storage dishes that she put in the cellar along with fresh buttermilk. "You must think the stew is good, the way you're shoveling it down," she told her father, smiling at him.

"It's excellent," he told her, returning the smile. "Your new husband will be very pleased with your cooking."

New husband. "If he ever wakes up," she answered jokingly.

Her father chuckled. "Maybe after a good rest he can get back to a normal life. *Both* of you can."

"You're probably anxious to go home to Mama and the boys."

"They'll be all right. They're closer to town. I'm mainly worried about your brother wanting to join the Continental Army. Luke can sure tell him he's got no idea what it's like killin' a man, even when the man's the enemy, let alone the fact that he could get himself killed in return." Henry dipped some fresh bread into the stew gravy. "It's a damn mess, all right, just like Luke said." He shoved the bread into his mouth. After swallowing, he continued. "Men like Jeremiah, things like that seem to come natural to them, like that there George Washington being in command of the whole Continental Army. Not every man will take on somethin' like that. They're a strange breed."

Annie thought about Jeremiah. Yes indeed, a strange breed. "I'll have Luke talk to Jake. Maybe that will help."

"Could be." Henry finished his stew and bread, then downed a large glass of buttermilk. "I'll sleep in the barn again," he told Annie, rising. "I'll leave you two to settle your own affairs, if indeed Luke wakes up." He walked around to give her a light hug. "Right now, I'll go finish chores. I won't come back inside till suppertime."

"Thanks, Pa, but you're working too hard. You look so tired, and you've been losing weight."

"Oh, I'll bounce back," he told her with a reassuring wink.

Annie suspected he felt worse than he let on. She loved him for helping out this way. He walked out the door, and she cleaned off the table, then scrubbed the dishes in a small washtub, leaving them out to dry. Taking a deep breath, she walked toward the bedroom. She had to sleep herself. She'd been up all night working on the bread, the butter, and the stew, as well as some mending. She'd been too worried about Luke to sleep, and she wanted her chores done when he woke up so that she could spend as much free time with him as possible.

She pondered the idea of lying down in the spare bedroom for now, not wanting to disturb Luke, yet she wondered if he might be upset if she didn't come to his bed. What would he want her to do?

She walked into the bedroom to get her flannel nightgown, only to notice to her surprise that Luke was finally awake. "Well! You're not dead after all!" She walked over to sit down on the edge of the bed. "Do you feel better?"

He studied her for a moment. "Some." He stretched. "How long have I been sleeping?"

"Over sixteen hours! You got back yesterday and have slept ever since."

He sighed and ran a hand through his thick hair, then reached out to her, looking her over. "Come to bed, Annie."

Her heart rushed faster, and she swallowed. "I need to change into my nightgown first, and I feel kind of silly even doing that. It's the middle of the day, Luke."

He looked her over again. "You don't need the nightgown, and I'm glad it's daylight. I want to see you. I want to feel you beside me. You're my wife, and it's time to make that true in every sense."

Annie felt all the nerve endings in her body. She stood up and began undoing the many buttons down the front of her dress. "All right." He was right. It was time. When she got to the last button, she glanced at him. "Can I . . . just this first time . . . can you not watch me?"

He smiled and turned over, and she could see he was completely naked. Her heart pounded as she finished undressing, then slipped into bed and pulled the covers over her nakedness. Luke turned to her, drawing her close, bare skin against bare skin.

"Luke—"

His mouth covered hers in a groaning kiss, and she felt his hardness against her. She wanted him. She loved him. She prayed he would never know about Jeremiah. Flashes from another time like this plagued her mind . . . another man . . . so like this one. Luke's strong hand moved over her bottom, around her thigh, exploring that secret place in much the same way Jeremiah had done, bringing her alive in a wonderful way that made her want him.

Luke. Right now, he was her whole world. Right now, he was the only man she wanted. In moments, she was crying out his name in a heated climax, so grateful he'd come home alive and unhurt, except for the scabbed gash at the side of his face, still puckered from her mother's stitches.

In the next moment, she gasped when Luke entered her with an almost harsh thrust in his want of her. Perhaps it was because it had been so long since Jeremiah did this, and because she'd shared only that one night with him, but the surge of Luke's swollen penis hurt her. Yet in spite of the initial pain, his continued thrusts brought out a wicked desire that made Annie dig her fingers into his muscled shoulders, wanting him to stop, yet wanting him to *never* stop. Was it right to want a man this way? With Jeremiah, it surely had been sinful. But Luke was her husband. Surely there was nothing wrong with desiring him this way.

Soon she felt the pulsing of his life deep inside. He kissed her neck, her throat, moving down to kiss her nipples, setting her on fire.

"I want to do it again," he whispered gruffly. "Did I hurt you?"

"I'll be all right, Luke. Do what you need to do. I love you, and I'm just so glad you're back." She leaned up and invited another kiss. "You'll stay now, won't you? You won't go off to war?"

Another kiss.

"I'll stay."

She arched up to greet him as he entered her again, this time more gently. Secretly, she prayed for Jeremiah, hoping that somehow he would find this kind of happiness for himself, and that no harm would come to him. For now . . . and forever . . . she belonged with Luke.

12

August 20, 1780
Deep Forest of the Ohio Valley

Jeremiah awoke to a crackling fire and the sweet smell of wood smoke. Through a smoke hole above him, he caught sight of a couple of twinkling stars.

So, it was night. Because of the smoke hole, he knew this must be a Delaware longhouse, or perhaps a smaller hut. Wincing against the pain any motion caused, he managed to turn his head to look around better, seeing that he indeed lay in a conical-shaped dwelling made of branches and mud. Although he expected the familiar pain in his side from his gunshot wound, a fierce pain in his neck and shoulders reminded him he'd suffered yet another wound during the Indian attack on the English soldiers. Gradually, he remembered a blow between his shoulder blades, but wasn't sure of what it was from—only that it sent him reeling and he'd blacked out. He hoped it had been something blunt and not a life-threatening injury from a tomahawk. He was almost afraid to try moving his limbs.

Luke! Was his brother all right? Had everything gone as planned? He couldn't remember seeing him. Fact was, he could remember nothing of the battle but the blow he'd taken.

He closed his eyes again, struggling to remember; but all he could recall was the painfully bumpy ride in the back of the wagon, four full days with little rest, little to eat or drink, and no medical attention . . . four full days of constant threats from Colonel Weatherford. The next thing he remembered was hearing screams and gunfire, whinnying horses, the sound of warriors' war whoops . . . then nothing.

He closed his eyes again, listening to the pop and crackle of the fire, thinking how peaceful it sounded. He summoned up enough courage to wiggle his hands and feet, and he breathed a sigh of relief that he could move them. Groaning, he moved his legs, and it was then he realized that he wore nothing under the blanket that covered him.

How long had he been lying here? Where was Luke? The wonder brought thoughts of Annie. Luke had probably gone home to her. He had to find out for sure. If something had happened to Luke, he had a responsibility to go back to Annie and tell her, see if she needed anything, comfort her, apologize . . . take care of her for Luke.

How did a man apologize for being responsible for the death of a new bride's husband? How did he apologize for destroying her entire future? How was it he managed to hurt the very people he cared most about?

Annie. Right now, Luke could be sharing his bed with her . . . claiming her as his own . . . enjoying the sweet pleasure of being inside her.

She was mine first, he reminded himself, reassuring his wounded male pride the only way he knew how. He wanted to shout that Annie Barnes belonged to him, but what good would that do? He was no kind of man for a woman like Annie. She would have been miserable married to him. Luke would soon win her over, heart, body, and soul. That was as it should be, but he would never forget her . . . nor would he ever stop wanting her.

He felt a cool draft and realized that someone had pulled back the heavy deerhide flap at the entrance of the hut. In the next moment, Jimmy Bear was kneeling beside him. The man was old enough to be Jeremiah's father, but he was agile and strong. Jeremiah had seen him fight with as much skill as any younger warrior.

"You are awake," the man stated, sitting down beside Jeremiah. "Shara has been tending you. The wound in your side broke open but did not seem infected. It is the blow to the back of your neck that made you sleep so long."

"How long is that?" Jeremiah asked, thinking he'd been out for only a few hours.

"It was four days ago that we helped you escape."

"Four days!" Jeremiah put a hand to his forehead, rubbing it. "What about my brother?"

"He got away unhurt, after we were sure all the Redcoat soldiers were dead. No one can be blamed for their deaths but the Iroquois. We are used to being blamed for things, even killings we have not committed. They might even think you were killed, too. Then they will stop looking for you."

Jeremiah sighed deeply. "I can't take that chance once I leave here. But I have good friends back East who will hide me, and once I get back into scouting for the Continental Army, I'll be among friends and soldiers. Things are coming to a climax, Jimmy Bear. I can sense it. Another year and I'll bet the United States will be independent of England. When that happens, England will pull out, and I'll be a free man."

"And what will happen to the Iroquois?"

Their gazes held. "I wish I knew, Jimmy Bear. The French

have never treated you fairly, nor the English . . . nor, I imagine, will the colonists. After all, they are the ones who keep pushing into Indian country."

"Including men like your brother."

Jeremiah rested his hands across his stomach. "I appreciate your people leaving the settlement at Willow Creek alone."

Jimmy Bear nodded. "You saved me once when white men tried to hang me, and you helped my people when you spoke on their behalf to the English soldiers who came to attack us long ago."

"Yeah, well, I won't be able to do any more of that, I'm afraid. I just hope you and the others here don't suffer for helping me."

"They cannot prove it was us who killed all those Redcoats. There are Shawnee around here, too, and of course, the Wyandots. By the time those waiting realize those soldiers are not coming back, the remains will be so rotted, they will not be sure just what happened."

Now Jeremiah remembered killing two of the soldiers himself. He could not remember seeing Luke, and after spending those last several days with him, he missed his brother. He wondered if Luke took part in any of the slaying. War was such an ugly thing. Luke had likely learned that firsthand. He couldn't help wondering if his brother would end up getting involved in the fighting himself. He hoped not, as that would leave Annie alone.

"I'll be leaving here as soon as I can," he told Jimmy Bear. "I'll go to Philadelphia and find out the latest news, maybe find George Washington and see what more I can do to help."

Jimmy Bear nodded. "The hard part for us will be when you white men stop fighting each other. Then more will start coming over the mountains into the Valley of the Bloody River to take more Indian land."

Jeremiah couldn't help feeling sorry for the man. "And the river will get bloodier."

Their gazes held in sorrowful understanding. "Yes," Jimmy Bear answered. "It is then that it might be well for your brother and the others to go even farther west, or go back to where they came from."

Jeremiah looked up at the smoke hole again. "They won't do that, Jimmy Bear. They've lived here too long now. My brother has a farm here. It's home to him. He'll likely stay and get rich selling supplies to those who *do* decide to head farther west." He looked back at Jimmy Bear. "There is no stopping it, my friend, no matter how hard you fight it. There are far too many whites on the other side of these mountains, many more than there are Iroquois of any clan. I've heard there is a great river that divides this country, much farther west from here, and I've seen some of the great lakes that also lie farther west. White men will want to go there and see these things for themselves, and take advantage of the great waterways, maybe even claim much of that land for the United States."

Jimmy Bear sighed. "They are like hungry wolves."

Jeremiah thought about Luke. "They are just doing what comes naturally," he told the Indian. "I am myself interested in going farther west." *The farther away from Luke and Annie the better,* he thought. *Once this war is over...*

"So many changes," Jimmy Bear told him. "It saddens my heart."

Jeremiah reached out and touched his arm. "No matter what the changes, Jimmy Bear, you will always be my good friend."

The Indian nodded. "And I yours." He suddenly smiled.

"And if you go west, Jeremiah, you should not go alone. You should have a woman with you. You know that my daughter Shara would be proud to be your woman. She is all grown-up now, and she thinks you are a fine specimen for a white man."

Jeremiah thought about how he'd hurt Annie. He didn't want to visit that same hurt on yet another sweet and caring young woman, but he had to smile at Jimmy Bear's strong hint. "I have too much to do yet," he answered the man. "I thank you for thinking me worthy of your honorable daughter, but I have no idea where I will be in the next few months, or if I'll live to return. Shara is too important to treat lightly. Besides, her true place is with a respected Delaware man. There must be several who want to win her hand."

Jimmy Bear chuckled. "Many. I will be a rich man by the time they all finish bringing gifts to impress me and Shara."

Both men laughed, but pain shot through Jeremiah, sobering him. Jimmy Bear pressed his arm. "You are safe here, Jeremiah. You may stay with us as long as it takes for you to heal."

"I'm grateful, Jimmy Bear. I'll be on my way as soon as possible."

"To fight the *white* man's war."

"Yes, to fight the white man's war."

13

September 5, 1780

Annie wiped at perspiration with the back of her hand. After a chilly start to the day, the afternoon had grown hot enough to cause a sweat at any kind of vigorous labor.

She looked down at her hands, scratched and callused, dirt so embedded in the creases of her dry skin she wondered if she'd ever be able to get it all out. Scrubbing them with lye soap only made them burn.

Normally, one of her brothers would have come to help Luke, but ever since English soldiers had arrived in their area, her father had not been well, heartbroken over the fact that Jake had run off to "find" George Washington and offer his services in the fight for freedom. Young Calvin was left to help his father with the blacksmithing, and because of a bout of arthritis, Annie's mother needed Sally's help at home.

Annie did not doubt that part of her father's sudden failing health was due to Jake going off to who-knew-where, possibly to get himself killed for reasons he didn't even understand, let alone the fact that Jake would be riding through hostile Indian country. Worry took its toll on the aged, and it showed in her father's thinning face and sudden loss of energy. She'd known Henry Barnes only to be strong and vigorous, and her mother had always managed to accomplish her daily chores in spite of her arthritis.

All that was changed now. Many things had changed since that fateful day of her wedding, six weeks ago. Nothing and no one had been the same. Just a few days ago, the survivor of an Indian attack at a settlement northwest of Willow Creek brought terrible news—Indian tribes were using the excuse of siding with the English to raid and murder at many settlements along the frontier. His story of what had happened at his own settlement was one of sheer horror, and her parents had begged Annie and Luke to come to Willow Creek and stay with them, where they would be safer, but Luke first wanted to get in his harvest. Because of Jeremiah's friendship with Jimmy Bear of the more friendly Delaware, he hoped for continued peace in their area.

All the changes and worry made it an effort even for Annie to keep up enough energy to manage her household chores as well as to help with the harvest. So far, she'd hidden her morning sickness from Luke. She didn't want him to know she might be pregnant until after all the corn and potatoes were harvested. He was at this moment digging potatoes while she picked corn. That made it easier to keep from him the fact that she vomited at least twice every morning.

She was thrilled to be giving Luke Wilde a child, and how could any woman not appreciate a man like Luke in her bed? They made love often, and with passionate pleasure, no matter how tired they felt. Still, the anxious circumstances under which they lived took some of the joy out of her pregnancy. Luke had enough to worry about right now without knowing his wife was carrying and shouldn't be out here lifting heavy bushels of corn. She did not want to be the reason he could not complete his harvest this year. She wanted to be strong for him, show him he'd married well. And getting in what was a bountiful harvest was so important.

Luke was good to her, so attentive, apologizing every night at supper that she had to do these extra chores. She assured him she didn't mind, but deep inside she knew why she was willing to do anything she could to please him. It was not just her love for him. It was the fact that she'd also loved his brother. Somehow, she felt she needed to make up for that by being the best wife a man could possibly ask for, and so she refused to complain about anything.

She carted another basket of corn to the waiting wagon. Luke would use part of the corn to feed his growing herd of cattle. The bulk of it and the potatoes would be sold to traders, who came through every year with large wagons to haul the produce east to Virginia. The wagons were always well-guarded against Indian attack. Whether the traders sold the goods to Tories or Patriots mattered little to Luke as long as he was well-paid. However, it would be difficult not to care this year. And for the past three years, there had been no guarantee that the traders would even show up.

"Annie?"

She set the bushel on the wagon and turned to see Luke approaching.

"You've done enough for today. Go inside and lie down."

"There is too much left, and even if I went to the house, there are plenty of chores to do there. I've let the wash pile up so that it will take me two days instead of one to get it all done."

Luke came closer and wrapped his arms around her. "I'll find someone to help you with it, I promise. I'm sorry this had to be the year I can't have any help. I didn't intend for you to have to work like this when you married me."

She breathed deeply of his scent, a mixture of fresh-dug earth and the sweat of a man who labored hard to provide for his own. "It's all right, Luke. I've always worked hard."

"Not this hard." He pulled back, grasping her shoulders. "I have a lot of money saved, Annie, enough that if I get what I should from the traders this year, I can afford to hire help next summer. Your only job will be to take care of the house . . . and maybe, by then, a baby."

She smiled, studying her husband's blue eyes. She considered telling him about the baby, but the harvest would be finished in only a few more days. She would wait. Luke leaned down and kissed her gently.

"Go to the house," he reiterated. "You're done here. And when harvest is finished, I'll fill that tin bathtub of mine with hot water and let you soak in it all day if you want."

"Now that I might allow," she returned with a smile.

He grasped her hands. "We'll get all the dirt out of these poor hands and I'll scrub your feet for you and—"

"Luke Wilde! You don't have to feel so guilty for how hard I work. And what about you? You've been working so hard that you've lost weight. When you come in later, I promise you'll be eating a full dinner of potatoes and gravy and pork and pie and fresh bread. God knows, you need to eat!"

He laughed, putting a hand to the side of her face. "I look forward to it. Now go!"

She grasped his wrist and kissed his hand. "If you say so." She headed for the house, and as she nearly reached the steps to the front porch, she heard a rider approaching. She turned to see. It was Clinton Thom, a good friend of her father's. He slowed his horse some as he came closer, then halted nearby. Lucifer barked and raced around the man's horse.

"Luke around?" Clint called to her.

Annie shouted to Lucifer to calm down, and before she could answer Clint, she saw Luke running toward them from the cornfield, musket in hand. These days, they had to always be ready for any kind of attack.

"What's up, Clint?" Luke shouted.

Clint dismounted, a tall string bean of a man whose head was actually higher than that of the horse he rode. He waited for Luke to reach them before speaking.

"Hate to be the bearer of bad news, Luke, but we got word today from long hunters who just came in from another settlement downriver. They say the place was laid waste by Tories, with the help of Wyandots. We can't expect to stay free of raids for much longer. Seems the Injuns are still on a real rampage, taking advantage of the war and all."

"Tories! How can white men attack innocents of their own kind just because they think we should all be loyal to a king thousands of miles away?"

Annie felt alarm at the words, still worried lest Luke go off himself over the winter to fight the English. Ever since the arrival of Weatherford's troops, Luke had stewed about the whole situation. He still bore a long white scar on his right cheek from the vicious blow Weatherford had given him.

"They say that in some cases, this war has come to be brother against brother and father against son," Clint answered. "Either way, Annie's pa wanted me to come out here and tell you the latest. On top of that—" The man glanced at Annie. "Sorry to tell you, ma'am, but your pa seems to be getting worse. Your ma thinks it's his heart—broke from Jake leaving, and now all this worry about Injuns and Tories. He just ain't been the same since them soldiers came to Willow Creek."

Annie closed her eyes and turned away. What was next? "Give him my love," she told Clint.

"You folks comin' in closer to town soon?" Clint asked Luke.

"I expect we'll have to for the winter," Luke answered.

Annie could feel his anger and disappointment. So far, nothing he'd planned for their living here had worked out. They had envisioned a much happier, more peaceful life, and Luke had worked so hard to build the house. He'd done so well here, all by his own backbreaking work.

"We have a harvest to finish," Luke told Clint.

"Don't be taking too long to do it," Clint answered. "I might be able to spare my younger son Billy. I can bring him out tomorrow if you want."

"I'd appreciate it, Clint. Annie is working much too hard."

"Well, if it will help you finish up sooner and get yourselves to safety, I'll bring him out then. Good-bye to you both."

Annie looked up as the lanky man climbed on his horse, his feet actually hanging close to the ground. He wore homespun clothing that was still dusty from his own harvesting.

"Thank you for taking time away from your farm to come out here," Annie told him.

Clint tipped his hat to them and rode off. Annie looked up at Luke, whose eyes showed both anger and sadness. "We'll get through this and live a good life, Annie Wilde," he told her.

Annie prayed inwardly with all her heart that his words would prove true. She turned to go inside, every muscle in her body aching for rest.

14

Jeremiah moved stealthily toward the campfire he'd smelled a good mile away. He left his horse tethered at a distance so he could more quietly approach the men around the fire, wanting first to know if they were friend or foe, white or Indian.

"... damned sons of bitches will find out they ought not to threaten us," one man swore.

Now he knew they were white. He kept his musket in hand, primed and ready. He'd won many a contest with other long hunters and mountain men wherein a man had to fill, prime, and load his musket while running, since such a feat was often handy in real-life situations for men who lived as he did. Neither Indians nor any other kind of enemy was going to give a man time to stop and reload when they were on his tail.

"Let them Tories come," another grumbled. "We'll make Ferguson eat his words."

Jeremiah knew the name. Major Patrick Ferguson was a leader of American Tories, men who could do just as much damage against Patriots and their families as English soldiers, or even

Indians. The men around the fire were surely Patriots, but by
their dress, they were definitely not part of the Continental Army.
They were rugged, bearded, mostly buckskin-clad mountain
men, many of them wearing beaver and coonskin hats. He knew
their type well. He *was* their type, but he'd always kept himself
clean-shaven. Raising his musket over his head, he made ready
to step into the clearing.

"Hello there!" he shouted first. "Friend coming in. I'm
alone."

Many of them quickly rose, readying their weapons. Jeremiah walked into the light of the fire, keeping his weapon high.
"Name's Jeremiah Wilde, and I'm a Patriot. From your talk, I'm
guessing you're the same."

Two of the eight men quickly left the circle, and Jeremiah
guessed they would scout out the perimeter of their camp to
make sure he truly was alone. A couple of the others lowered
their weapons, but the apparent leader of the men kept his gun
leveled on Jeremiah.

"You won't mind if we relieve you of that long gun while
we get to know you, will you?" the man asked.

"Not at all." Jeremiah slowly lowered the gun and handed
it butt-first to one of the others. "I've been looking for someone
involved in the war so I can find out the latest news. I've been
laid up wounded for about a month and I'm not sure what's
happening."

The leader spat out part of a wad of tobacco before motioning to Jeremiah to sit down. "My name's Ralph Higgins, and
these here are my friends."

He looked Jeremiah over as Jeremiah took a seat on a fallen
log. Other than the crackling fire, the camp hung quiet as the
rest of the men studied Jeremiah. Cold nights had begun to quiet

the frogs, and many birds had already taken off for parts even farther south. Here in the Blue Ridge Mountains of the western Carolinas, things were even colder and quieter. There were few night sounds now other than the occasional hoot of an owl and the cry of a mountain lion.

"How do we know we can trust you, or that you're not a spy for the Tories?" Higgins asked.

Jeremiah shrugged. "Guess you'll just have to take my word for it. I can tell you my father was good friends with George Washington before I was even born, and I befriended Washington when this war first started. Then I spent some time as a captive on an English ship. I escaped, and English soldiers caught up with me, which is how I was wounded. How I got out of that is a long story. I also heard you talking about Major Patrick Ferguson. I know enough about this mess to know he's a leader of Tories. What's he got to do with all of you camping here tonight?"

"The bastard—"

"Shut up, Terrence!" Higgins told the man who'd started to speak. "We still don't know if we can trust this man."

Jeremiah eyed all of them. Any one of them could likely give him a run for his money. These were seasoned men, perfect for fighting Tories, if indeed that's what they were about. He turned his gaze back to Higgins. "You're a wise man. I'd feel the same if I were you. A man doesn't know who he can trust these days." He leaned forward, resting his elbows on his knees. "I used to carry a letter from George Washington himself stating I was a Patriot and a good friend, but that was taken from me after the English arrested me as a traitor. I guess the only proof I have left is to show you my back."

Higgins frowned. "Your back? Why's that?"

Jeremiah stood up, removing the wolfskin coat he wore, then untying and removing his buckskin shirt. He turned his back to the light of the fire.

"Jesus!" one man exclaimed.

"God Almighty," another murmured.

"How'd you get them scars?" Higgins asked.

"Can you read?" Jeremiah asked. "The ones across the middle of my back were carved on top of the lashing. I don't know how clear they are now, but they spell TRAITOR. The English did that to me after I was arrested. I spent the next two years as a slave on one of their warships. How I escaped is my business, but I can tell you I have a ripe hatred for the English *and* the Tories." He showed them the scar from his gunshot wound. "An English soldier did this to me, too." He put his shirt and coat back on.

"Give the man some coffee," Higgins told one of the others.

Jeremiah could see they all looked at him with a new respect.

"Return the man's musket, Logan," Higgins told yet another man. He moved closer to Jeremiah and put out his hand. "Glad to meet you, Patriot."

Jeremiah grinned and shook his hand. "So, do you mind telling me what's going on here?"

Higgins spat yet another round of tobacco juice before replying. "Don't mind at all, especially if you mean to join us. You look like a man who can handle his weapons."

Jeremiah took a tin cup of hot coffee from one of the others, then drank some, thinking if it was any stronger, it would be solidified. Still, he liked his coffee strong, and its warmth felt good going down. "I do all right," he told Higgins. "I'd be willing to take on any man here in a run-and-shoot contest . . . for the right amount of money, of course."

Higgins and the others laughed.

"I'll take you up on that one," the man called Terrence told Jeremiah.

Jeremiah grinned and nodded, turning back to Higgins. "So, what would I be joining you in doing?"

"We're headed toward the Cowpens to join up with the Continental Army and then on to King's Mountain to make a stand against Patrick Ferguson and his Tories. He's got about a thousand men, but we've sent word by runners to gather up more mountain men, farmers, hunters, blacksmiths, folks of all backgrounds that are hardy men who've lived in these mountains for years and know how to fight. We've all stove off Injuns most of our lives, and we can take on the likes of Ferguson and them who dare to threaten their own kind." The man spat again. "Logan over there, he was once a prisoner of Ferguson and his men. Ferguson released him in order to come tell us to disband and give up the Patriot cause, or he'll march his army over these mountains and hang our leaders and burn our settlements. We don't none of us take kindly to bein' threatened. We intend to make Ferguson regret his words."

Jeremiah nodded. "Sounds like a good idea to me. I've been eager to get back into the fight, but I wasn't sure where to head first. I had a suspicion things were going to get heavy to the south, which is why I headed in this direction after I left the Ohio Valley. I'd gone there to visit family."

"Glad to have you aboard. We're headed for Quaker Meadows to meet up with more of our friends before we go on to the Cowpens. You got a horse?"

Jeremiah nodded. "I left him yonder a ways. I'd better get back to him before he becomes a meal for a mountain lion."

Higgins chuckled. "I agree. When you get back, you're welcome to a strip of jerked meat and biscuits hard enough to break your teeth, if you don't mind the worms inside."

Jeremiah rose, grinning. "There have been times when I've had to feast on worms alone," he answered. "The bread wrapped around them will just make them tastier."

The others laughed again as Jeremiah left the fire to get his horse. It felt good to be back in the fight. Keeping busy might help him stop worrying so much about Luke and Annie . . . and stop thinking about how much he still loved his brother's wife.

15

September 20, 1780

Luke leaned back in the wooden rocker, taking a deep breath and patting his stomach. "I suppose you know I'm going to get fat being married to such a good cook," he told Annie. "I hope you won't mind."

Annie smiled, thinking of how weary she was as she walked over to sit down on his lap. "As hard as you've worked, I hardly think you'll be getting fat anytime soon."

He chuckled, putting his arms around her as she rested her head on his shoulder. "Now that harvest is finished, I'll be a lot less active over the winter."

Annie kissed his cheek and nestled against him. "I don't think so. There's still a lot of wood to be cut and hauled and split, and animals to be fed through the winter, and—"

"Please!" he interrupted. "Let me enjoy a *few* days of rest! Give me some time to revel in the fact that we actually finished bringing everything in, the cellar is full, with two wagons packed to take into Willow Creek, and more stacked up for a second trip. And now I will have more time to dote on my poor neglected wife." He turned his head to kiss her.

Annie moved her arms around his neck, returning the kiss. "I don't feel neglected," she told him as his kisses moved to her throat. "Just very, very tired."

Again his lips moved to her mouth for another kiss, after which he answered her. "Then leave for tomorrow whatever chores you have left. Thank God your mother was able to come out and help you with the laundry a few days ago. Whatever you have now we will take into town with us tomorrow and you and your mother can do laundry there together." He lifted her hand and kissed its rough redness. "My God, Annie, I've got to hire more help next year."

"Don't fret about it, Luke." Annie sat up a little straighter. "I *do* agree, but not for the reason you think." She took a deep breath before continuing. "I may not be able to help next season because I'll be watching after our baby." She watched his smile fade, and then near horror come into his handsome blue eyes.

"Baby!" He looked her over, frowning. "You're carrying?"

Annie smiled and nodded.

"You should have *told* me! I *never* would have allowed you to work so hard, Annie!" He picked her up in his arms and rose, then set her in the chair. He began pacing then, running a hand through his hair.

"Luke, I'm fine. If something is going to go wrong with things, it will happen no matter what. We can only pray this child inside me is meant to be born and live a good, long time. I'm just happy I'm carrying."

Luke looked her over lovingly. "How do you feel?"

Annie shrugged. "I've been sick mornings, but that's how it usually is."

"Does your mother know?"

"No. I wanted you to be first, and I wanted to make sure I got through harvest time."

Luke finally grinned, shaking his head. "Let's think boy. I'd love a son."

Annie walked over to hug him. "I have a feeling a little girl would suit you just fine, too. She'd have you running at her beck and call, Luke Wilde."

He pressed her close, kissing her hair. "I don't doubt that. I hope Jeremiah comes back after this damned war is over so he can see his new niece or nephew."

"Oh, I hope so, too, Luke. I pray for him every day."

"Well, in the meantime, I don't care *how* good you feel," Luke told her then. "From now on, I am going to find you help for some of your chores."

"Luke, keeping extra people around would be expensive."

"I can afford it now. And it will be worth it to keep you and my son or daughter healthy. Until we have a whole brood of kids and the older ones can help, then we'll need that help from the outside." He hugged her close again. "I'm so happy about the baby, Annie."

"Well, I'm happy that *you're* happy." They both laughed, still hugging when suddenly the door was violently kicked open.

Annie let out a little scream as she jumped away, and quickly Luke shoved her behind him as several men in black boots, homespun pants, and animal-skin coats barged into the house. Mingled among them were painted Indians, who in spite of the cold night were naked from the waist up, except for their paint. Several sported rings and pieces of tin hanging from holes in their ears, lips, and noses. Some were covered with tattoos.

Luke dived for his musket, always kept primed and ready, but a knife whirred across the room and landed in his shoulder.

"Luke!" Annie screamed as he staggered. She reached out to him, but in that quick moment, one of the tattooed Indians rushed forward and grabbed her.

Annie fought wildly, bashing the back of her head against the Indian who held her, using her fingernails, kicking, biting. Nothing helped.

"Luke!" she screamed over and over, but several of the white men stood around him, kicking and beating him. "Stop! Stop!" she screamed. Indians and white men alike began destroying everything in the house, including the beautiful hutch Luke had built with his own hands and the china inside it, her cherished wedding gift. The hand-built table was overturned and chopped to pieces. Ashes from both fireplaces were swept into the room, causing a black cloud of filth to spread over everything. Curtains were ripped down and bedding torn apart, then set afire.

Luke and Annie were dragged outside. Annie's abductor pressed a huge hunting knife against her cheek as he propelled her down the steps. The men forcing Luke through the door threw him to the ground. He appeared to still be conscious, but he bled profusely from his bruised and battered face. Painted, half-naked Indians screamed and whooped as the house began to burn brighter—the beautiful stone house Luke had labored so hard and so long to build for his bride.

Flames were already licking at the wooden upper story, while Luke and Annie were dragged toward the barn, where stored piles of feed were already ablaze. Animals were shot, chickens chased down. Indians gleefully ripped the heads off the chickens, and feathers flew everywhere. Luke rallied and tried to fight, managing to throw off one man and land a foot in another man's belly, but soon several men again were upon him. Annie was sure she would see him chopped to pieces by the Indians, as was probably her own fate, but strangely, the Indians did not take part in the beatings. They screeched and danced and laughed as instead, they focused on destroying everything in sight, while only the white men abused Annie and Luke.

Next came the precious harvested corn. The two wagons carrying corn and potatoes were set afire. Some of the white men quickly gathered some of the food and threw it in sacks for themselves. Annie was so stunned she couldn't even be sure of how many had attacked, nor was she sure of why. Extra harvested corn stacked beside the barn was set on fire, as was the barn itself. Indians chased out Luke's fine horse, and one leaped on its back and rode off on it. It was only then that Annie noticed Lucifer lying nearby, the dog's head cut off.

"Lucifer!" she cried, again trying to wrench herself free, but the Indian who held her wrenched her arm behind her, nicking her throat with his hunting knife. She ached to go to Luke. Luke! Just moments ago, they were so happy . . . so happy.

Now the apparent leader of the white men ordered the Indian holding her to pull her closer to Luke. There she was kicked in the back and fell near her husband, who rolled back and forth in pain.

"We should kill you!" the bearded, buckskin-clad leader shouted to them. "But it is better punishment to let you see the destruction that awaits those who supply the traitorous Patriots!" the man told them. He leaned down and grasped the front of Annie's dress, ripping it downward.

Annie screamed and quickly pulled up the garment to cover her breasts. She crawled closer to Luke.

"Annie," he groaned. "My Annie." He reached over, as though to protect her, but one of the other white men kicked him again.

"Luke!" Annie again tried to crawl to him, but then came a crashing blow to the back of her head. In a semiconscious daze, she felt her body being dragged somewhere, felt her clothes ripped off. She tried to see, but when she opened her eyes, there was only blackness. She felt the horrid touches, the ugly penetrations. Yet it was as though it was an awful nightmare, not really happening to her. She caught words here and there—"Patriot bitch," "teach him a lesson," "Hagan was right."

Hagan? Who was Hagan? Surely not Luke's neighbor, John Hagan. He'd helped build the very barn that now was being burned to the ground! It was only then that Annie realized John Hagan had not attended her wedding, was not present when the English soldiers came. He'd been angry over Jeremiah's return to Willow Creek. Was he the one who'd somehow summoned the English soldiers? Was he the one who'd instigated this horrible raid?

How odd that she could keep her thoughts on the man, trying to figure out why Luke and the farm had been attacked . . . while all the time, men were taking turns with her. She felt totally unattached from her body and her emotions. Perhaps she was dying and her spirit was lifting away, separated from the ugly reality of what was happening to her and all around her.

She could smell smoke, felt cold. Yes. Cold. She was lying naked. She could tell that, even though she still couldn't see anything. She knew instinctively that the attack was over. She heard horses, war whoops, laughter, victorious yelling.

"Leave them!" someone shouted. "When they come around, they will see the cost of supporting the Patriots! And the traders we killed won't be coming for their harvest; even if they could, there will be nothing here for them. If we're lucky, they'll all die of starvation. Let's head to Willow Creek!"

More shouts, and the sound of thundering horses' hooves. Funny that she and Luke had not heard those horses coming in the first place. She wondered what tribe the Indians were, but then, what did it matter? Revolution or no revolution, Patriots or Tories, the Indians were always a worrisome threat, for their own reasons.

Finally, the only sound was the crackling of fire, the crashing of what she supposed must be the roofs of the house and barn coming down. *Luke! His beautiful farm! His hard-earned harvest! Our home! The animals! Lucifer! How could everything have been so wonderful, so beautiful, so happy, such a short time ago? Why has God allowed this awful thing to happen? Where is Luke? Have they killed him after all?*

Now she felt a cold rain, icy drops of water stinging her skin. She didn't know if she should move or lie still. Maybe she wasn't even really alive. After all, she couldn't be sure what death was like. And since she couldn't see a thing, perhaps she was really dead and her spirit simply was having trouble letting go, probably because of Luke.

Suddenly she felt a wrenching pain deep in her belly and groin. It was so fierce it roused her, bringing her to the reality that yes, she was alive. She cried out, curling up on her side. The baby! Was she losing her precious baby? It seemed only moments ago that she was telling Luke she was having his child.

Luke! She summoned strength from some deep, dark depth she never knew existed in her soul and managed to cry out his name. "Luke! Luke!"

She felt a hand on her face. "Annie," someone groaned. "Oh, my God! What . . . have they done to you! Oh, God, Annie! Annie!"

Annie felt his body come over hers, apparently an effort to keep the rain off her and to keep her warm.

"Luke," she murmured, before all consciousness left her.

16

Annie had no idea of how long she lay unconscious. When she became aware of her surroundings again, she realized that someone was carrying her. She could hear rain falling; but again when she opened her eyes, she saw nothing. It took her a moment to remember . . . remember . . .

"Luke!" she cried out.

"It's . . . okay," she heard him answer. His voice was close. He was carrying her. ". . . have to . . . get you help."

"Luke . . . you're alive!"

He stopped, and she felt herself being lowered, heard him groan as he laid her on the ground. "Found . . . an old blanket . . . that didn't get burned." She felt his hand touch her face, felt him lean closer, felt him kiss her eyes. "Are you . . . warm enough?"

"Luke, where are we?" she moaned.

"About . . . halfway to . . . Willow Creek. I just hope . . . there are people left there . . . to help you. I'm getting you there . . . as fast as I can." He stroked her hair. "I think . . . I have broken ribs . . . God knows what else."

More memories came flooding in. The house burned! The harvest destroyed! Lucifer killed! The chickens! The animals! The new barn! Luke! They'd beaten him so savagely. How in God's name would he be able to carry her a whole mile into town? Such a strong, brave man. If only she could see his face! "Luke!" she cried. "My God, Luke, I can't see! I can't see!"

"It's all right," he tried to assure her. "You took . . . a nasty blow to the back of your head. It's probably . . . just temporary."

She felt him leaning closer again.

"Oh, my God, Annie! What they did to you! My God! My God! I'm so sorry! I should have been able . . . to protect you! Protect the baby!"

Baby! The pain in her belly. She still felt terrible cramps. Had she lost the baby? Now the worst memory of all came crashing down on her. Men touching her. Men saying ugly things. Men groping, ripping off her clothes, pulling her legs apart. She rolled to her side and vomited.

The baby was gone. She knew without asking. Her belly was empty. In a matter of perhaps twenty minutes, her world had been turned upside down, and it might never right itself. The happiness she and Luke had shared had been ripped to shreds. Everything Luke had worked for over the years was gone. The baby was gone. Perhaps Luke could never even love her in the same way again.

"Annie," he said, managing to again lift her. "I'll get you help. Don't die on me, Annie. You're all I have left."

She curled against him, unable to stop the screams that came up from her gut, through her throat, and out of her mouth, much like the very vomit she'd expelled a moment ago.

"Annie—" He put her down again.

"No! No! No!" she screamed. "My baby! Oh, God, Luke, they made me lose my baby! Those filthy murderers! God damn them! Damn them! Damn them!" She drew up her knees, shivering into the blanket, unable to think of anything for relief from the physical and emotional pain and horror but to scream and scream. Why had this happened? Why?

Luke held her tightly. "I'll find them," he told her. "I'll find them, and they will pay! I won't forget their faces! I won't forget what they did to us! I'm so goddamn sorry, Annie!"

Why was he sorry? He was only one man against perhaps twenty or thirty. There was nothing he could have done. And now there was nothing she could do but weep. Perhaps her tears would wash away whatever it was that kept her from seeing.

"You have to calm down . . . for now, Annie," Luke told her. "I have to . . . get you someplace warm . . . get you cleaned up . . . get help."

She felt him lift her yet again, heard him groan with his own pain. Only a man like Luke would be able to rise above his own terrible injuries to get help for her instead. She continued crying, more quietly now, as she rested her head on his shoulder while he began walking again. She felt more rain on her face, realized then that his neck was wet. He was carrying her in a cold rain, probably freezing himself, injured, angry, heartbroken. Would their love survive this horror? Could life ever be the same? All these years, they had avoided the ugly side of the war going on all around them. Somehow, it had seemed it would never really touch their lives. Now it had come roaring in upon them with all its fierce ugliness.

Patriots. Tories. English soldiers. Indians. Loyalists. It was all senseless. She remembered one of the attacker's words. *Hagan was right.* What did it all mean? Should she tell Luke? What would he do? Where would they go?

"Luke . . . let me walk. You can't carry me . . . all that way."

"Yes I can. You have no shoes, no clothes. You can't see."

"You'll kill yourself."

"I'll make it. I'd gladly die helping you live."

Annie winced against more cramps in her abdomen, deciding now she had to be stronger. She had to keep quiet so as not to alarm Luke any more than he already suffered. He was being so strong for her. She had to do the same for him. Surely he was in terrible pain himself. His face must be a bloody mess, and he'd said he thought he might have broken ribs. A rib could puncture his lung or his heart at any moment and kill him. Yet he managed to continue walking . . . in the cold rain . . . his heart surely exploding with grief. He had to be in agony over what had happened to his farm . . . their home . . . his dog.

Annie felt consciousness slipping away again. The back of her head throbbed. She'd been in so much abdominal pain that only then did she realize how much her head ached. She could only pray that Luke was right about her blindness, that it was only temporary.

She heard Luke panting now. How much longer could he keep this up? Blackness enveloped her again, and she felt herself floating out of his arms and back to earlier in the day, when she sat on his lap telling him about the baby, celebrating the harvest, sitting next to a warm fire . . .

17

September 22, 1780
The Cowpens, South Carolina

Jeremiah waited for orders. He and Ralph Higgins and his men were gathered at a place a few miles west of King's Mountain called the Cowpens because it was used for cattle roundups. Scouts had reported that Major Patrick Ferguson was taking a stance at King's Mountain, an odd, high, wooded piece of ground that looked out of place amid the more open farmland of western South Carolina. Apparently, Ferguson thought it a strategic point, a place where he could easily hold his ground.

Jeremiah and the others meant to prove the man wrong. Jeremiah was itching for a fight now, hoping to get this war over with, although he wasn't sure why. At one time, it would have been so that he could get back to Willow Creek; but there was no sense in that now, with Luke and Annie happily married. Fact was, he wasn't quite sure just what he would do when the fighting was done. Maybe he would scout for pilgrims who might want to settle even farther west than the Ohio Valley. Besides, he still intended to see all the land surrounding the Great Lakes.

Still more mountain men joined them at the Cowpens, as

regular militia, most of them in uniform but looking tired and hungry. Jeremiah figured there had to be up to a thousand men here. Scouts claimed Ferguson had roughly the same number of men, but the Patriots had an advantage. Ferguson would have a hard time holding King's Mountain for the simple reason that the lower area was thick with woods and brush. The Tories would be hard-pressed to find and hit their targets. The woods would give the Patriots plenty of cover as they ascended the hill to chase out the Tories. These mountain men would indeed make Ferguson "eat his words" about laying their country to waste. Ferguson had made a poor decision by settling in at the top of that mountain.

Jeremiah lit his pipe and drew on the sweet tobacco, thinking again about Annie while his horse gently grazed. She was surely the happy wife now, cooking for Luke, doing his wash and mending, baking his bread, sharing his bed.

His thoughts were interrupted by the approach of Ralph Higgins, who trotted his horse closer, looking grave. "The militia who just arrived had a story to tell," he told Jeremiah. "The name don't mean much to me, but they claim it's a really important piece of news, important to the war and to George Washington."

"What name?" Jeremiah asked. "What news?"

"Ever hear of a man called Benedict Arnold?"

Jeremiah frowned. "Hell yes. General Arnold was the commanding officer at West Point last I knew. He's a good friend of Washington's."

Higgins grinned. "Not anymore. The new men to arrive claim a man was caught up near Tarrytown carrying papers that showed the whole layout of West Point, some man named Andre. Come to find out this Andre was a spy sent by Benedict Arnold to carry the papers to the English, I guess to help them take

West Point. That could cut the states in two, if you could manage a blockade there."

Jeremiah thought for a moment, letting the news sink in. "Arnold? A traitor?" It didn't seem possible! The man was well liked by Washington and other Patriot leaders. He'd even done a lot to help the American cause. "Why would Arnold suddenly turn traitor?"

Higgins shrugged. "Who knows? Maybe the English made him an offer he couldn't turn down. Greed can make a man do a lot of things."

Jeremiah shook his head in disbelief. A man didn't know who to trust anymore. "Washington mentioned once something about Arnold feeling underused and unappreciated, had a problem with his ego. This betrayal must have made Washington furious. If it was me, I'd want to kill him with my bare hands!"

"I feel the same. They say the man named Andre will be shot or hanged. I guess Arnold managed to slip away to an English ship and hasn't been caught."

Jeremiah puffed his pipe in thought. "Well, I'd sure like to be the man to catch him!" he answered. "He'd not live long enough for a trial or an execution. I'd give him my own trial and execution right then and there."

Higgins chuckled. "Meantime, the new arrivals say we'll be trainin' here for a week or two before goin' on to King's Mountain to teach Ferguson and his Tories a right good lesson. They'll soon find out the mistake they made holin' up there, and especially the mistake they made in threatenin' us mountain men."

Jeremiah nodded. "Glad to help out. I expect I'll be heading for Virginia after this, see if I can find George Washington himself, if he's not still in New York. I'd like to talk to him about Ben Arnold."

"Well, that's my other bit of news. Didn't you say you had family over in the Ohio Valley?"

Jeremiah nodded, taking alarm. "I have a brother there."

"Well, the new arrivals say they captured some Loyalists northwest of here near Elizabethton and learned they was plannin' to head farther west—mostly just raiders lookin' for an excuse to rape and plunder the less-guarded settlements throughout the valley. Thought you'd want to know that."

Annie! Jeremiah felt a sudden pain in his gut. "Good thing they were caught before they could make good on their plans."

The regulars began shouting orders and organizing their men. There was no more time to talk . . . or to contemplate the information Higgins had just given him. Jeremiah pulled on his horse's reins to stop the gelding from grazing. He mounted and urged the animal into a light trot beside Higgins. Both men fell into formation with several other mountain men, riding behind the regular soldiers and heading for a larger gathering in the distance.

Jeremiah couldn't help worrying about what kind of danger Luke and Annie might be in. Maybe he should go back to Willow Creek and make sure they were all right. His head ached from torn loyalties, and the news about Benedict Arnold only made his confusion worse. Arnold had been a good friend and ally. Knowing a man like that had turned on them was disconcerting, to say the least. War certainly did affect a man in surprising ways.

18

September 23, 1780
Willow Creek

Annie stirred, hearing a young girl crying. She struggled to think who it could be, where she was. She thought for a moment, vaguely remembering Luke carrying her, being cold and wet. She opened her eyes to darkness, and in moments, the awful truth hit her. She was still blind!

"Luke!" she cried out.

"I'm right here, Annie."

There was his comforting voice—so close—but she could not see him. "I still can't see! I can't see!" She felt his gentle hand cover her eyes.

"Try not to panic. I just thank God you're alive, Annie...that we're *both* alive." He grasped her hand, and she felt him kiss it. "I love you, Annie. You've lost the baby, and...God knows how badly those bastards abused you! I'll make up for it, Annie. I'll make them pay!"

Her heart beat faster with dread at the words. "How? What do you mean, Luke? Don't leave me! Don't leave me when I can't see! And the baby! We've lost the baby! We've lost *every-*

thing! Everything! I couldn't bear to lose you, too . . . unless . . ."

He kissed her hand again. "Unless what?"

Her breath came in short gasps of shock and trauma. "You don't love me anymore. You don't want me anymore because of . . . what happened."

"Stop it!" He squeezed her hand almost painfully. "My love for you will *never* change!" She heard a choking sound. He suddenly let go of her hand, and she could tell he was himself fighting tears. She felt him rise, heard him pacing. "I can't let this go, Annie. I'll go *crazy* if I don't do something about it! A man is a man, and he has to do what he has to do. I have to try to find them, Annie. If I can't, I have to get involved in this war and at least kill a few Tories myself to get rid of the sick feeling in my *gut!*"

Annie put a hand to her face. "My God," she whispered. "Where are we, Luke?" she asked louder.

"At your parents'." She heard him come back and sit down near her. "I've been sitting by your side for nearly forty-eight hours, waiting for you to wake up. And here I am practically yelling at you. I'm so sorry, Annie! I'm so mixed up, so full of hate and vengeance. Now I know how Jeremiah felt about that whipping!"

Jeremiah. She hadn't thought about him since . . . she wasn't sure. What would he think of all this? He'd probably be ready to fight back right beside Luke. "Mother and Father . . . I remember those men saying something about Willow Creek. Did they come here?"

She heard Luke sigh as though in agony. "Yes. Apparently they somehow got the idea that this whole town was full of Patriots. By the time I got here with you, it was all over. They burned—" He suddenly gasped in what sounded to Annie like pain.

"Luke? Are you all right? Surely you're hurt."

He groaned lightly. "I'll live." He grasped her hand again. "They burned the supply store, your dad's blacksmith shed. Miraculously, your parent's house was spared, but they killed most of the chickens and cows, and . . . your brother . . . Calvin."

"Calvin!" Annie felt a piercing ache in her chest. "He was only fifteen!"

"Old enough to carry a musket, or so the Tories said. They ransacked the town, killed a lot of livestock, destroyed supplies people had brought in to trade. I remember them saying something about traders when they attacked our place. They must have come across men headed here to buy our supplies, and those men must have been buying for the Patriots."

Luke kissed her hand and remained quiet for the next several seconds. Annie was in such shock, and there were so many things to grieve for, that she hardly felt anything at all. Terror over her blindness consumed all other feelings, until she felt new alarm at Luke's sudden silence.

"Luke? What else is there? Is there more you're not telling me?"

He sighed deeply, the sigh of a man deeply burdened. "I'm afraid . . . this whole thing was too much for your father. He collapsed and died after Cal was killed, more over the horrible way he died than the death itself."

Annie felt nauseous. "How did he die?"

"You don't want to know."

Annie pulled away from him and turned on her side. "My God," she groaned. "My brother. My father. And God knows what's happened to Jake . . . or to your own brother. Luke, I don't feel real. I can't comprehend all of this. I can't *believe* all of this! Maybe if I could see . . . or if I could . . ." She curled up, and then the tears came in torrents. Calvin! Pa! And what would her mother and sister do now? What would she and Luke do? And the baby! The baby! It was gone! And those men! How much was one human being supposed to take? The thought of those men touching her, raping her, made her want to vomit again.

She felt Luke crawl onto the bed, felt his arms come around her from behind, felt him press against her. He embraced her tightly, resting the side of his face against her own.

"We have to be strong, Annie, very, very strong. You especially."

He held her while she wept, and wept, so hard and so long that it felt like her head would explode. Was there any one event of the past three days that required more tears than another? Now she understood why she'd heard her little sister crying. And her mother. Her poor mother! What awful grief she must be feeling. Was any one person's grief any more intense than another's? This was not something that could be compared to anything else. The only salve to any of their grief was the fact that most likely everyone in Willow Creek had reason to grieve— over lost fortunes, lost loved ones. Perhaps she was not the only woman who'd been . . . raped. Such an ugly word! Could Luke ever love her the same again? Did it even matter now?

"Annie, try to calm down. All your crying won't help your injuries."

"How can I *not* cry? Oh, God, Luke. Tell me you still love me!"

He kissed her cheek. "How can you even ask that? Nothing could stop me from loving you. Nothing."

"I'm so scared, Luke. What if I'm permanently blind?"

"I refuse to believe that. You have a head injury. It will heal. In the meantime, I'll be right here by your side. I'll get you and your mother and sister to safety at Fort Harmar. Several others

are going there, too. For the time being, we have to get what's
left of the women and children someplace safer."

Annie drew a deep breath, trying to think. The way he told
her about Fort Harmar made it sound like . . . "Luke, what will
you do when we get there?"

He remained silent again, and Annie could almost feel his
rage.

"Luke, answer me! What are you planning?"

He moved away from her. "I cannot and will not forgive
those men," he answered. His voice had a different tone to it
now. All the tenderness was gone. "I mean to find them and
make them pay!"

Annie covered her face and turned onto her back. "Don't
say it, Luke. Don't you dare say you're going to leave me."

"You'll be safe at Fort Harmar."

"No, Luke!"

"I don't have any choice! I can't just wait around there for
this war to end. It could take a year, maybe longer. They took
everything precious to me, Annie. *Everything!* I can't let that go
unanswered. The farm is destroyed, and even if it wasn't, I can't
replant till spring anyway. Winter is coming. I can't rebuild, and
even if and when I do, it will take every dime I had saved. There
will be no money coming this year from selling my harvest, because there's no harvest to sell!"

Annie could hear him pacing. She'd never, in all the years
she'd known Luke Wilde, heard or felt such anger out of him.
He suddenly reminded her more of Jeremiah.

"Luke, please, please don't go. Please don't leave me!"

"I wouldn't for a second if I didn't know you'd be safe and
if you wouldn't be with loved ones. You'll have your mother to
look after you until you get your sight back, and you *will* get

your sight back, do you hear me? You *will!* In the meantime, you'll have time to rest and heal, and you'll have Sally and your mother."

"And what if you get killed and never come back?" she nearly screamed at him.

"I won't get killed," he growled. "I'll be *doing* the killing! I'm going to look for Jeremiah while I'm at it. When he finds out what happened here, he'll *gladly* help me find those men and kill every last one of them."

Annie's grief became so consuming she wanted to scream. Her blindness only made it a hundred times worse. She felt trapped and terrified.

"I never knew . . . you had this side to you," she sobbed.

"Well, neither did I . . . until *now*. I've tried to stay out of this war, but now it has come to me uninvited. Someone has to pay for this, Annie. I'll go crazy if I don't do something to avenge this."

"And I'll go crazy if you leave!"

Another moment of silence. Annie heard him come closer again, felt him sit down on the bed. Again he took her hand.

"Annie, one thing I believe with all my heart is that you are the strongest, bravest woman I've ever known. We will make it through this, and after it's over, our love will be stronger than ever. Somehow we'll start over, and I'll still find a way to give you the kind of life I intended to give you. We'll have more babies, Annie. We'll build another home. We'll plant new crops. We'll find a way to get through this."

"Together, Luke. *Together!* Not apart!"

"Together in spirit. I'll never feel like a whole man again if I don't do this. I'll never feel like a proper husband. I can't *be* a proper husband again if I don't at least try to find those men. At the least, I can fight other Tories and show them that all they've done is make men like me and Jeremiah stronger and more determined. Now I understand better the Patriot cause. Now I understand that I have to do my share to win freedom for people like us. Please understand, Annie. I have to do this."

For that one black moment, Annie almost wished she'd been among those who'd died in the attack. She loved him, yet she wanted to hate him for leaving her in her darkest hour. She turned away, closing her eyes so she could pretend she wasn't really blind. She wanted to cry out to God, ask Him why He had let this happen to her . . . to all of them. Where was she to find the courage she would need?

"Do what you have to do," she told him. She couldn't help wondering if his leaving would end up like Jeremiah's. Maybe he'd be gone for years. Or maybe neither man would ever come back.

19

"They're up there all right!" Ralph Higgins spat brown tobacco juice to the ground as if he was spitting on the Tories and Loyalists at King's Mountain.

"Strange name for nothing more than an unusually steep hill," Jeremiah commented. "I wouldn't exactly call this a mountain."

A shot rang out from above, and a piece of pine branch fell to the ground nearby.

"With these trees for cover, Ferguson ain't got a chance," Higgins observed with a wry smile.

Jeremiah nodded, musket ready. They both waited while the rest of the Continentals and mountain men hurried to form a circle around the jutting piece of land that protruded from the surrounding flat farmland as though misplaced by nature. Somewhere from a distance, he heard shouting, more shots.

"They're probably tryin' to—"

Higgins's words were cut off by a crashing sound nearby. A dark-coated Loyalist soldier came bounding down the hill, a bayonet attached to his long rifle. He turned and saw Jeremiah and Higgins, and before he could react, Jeremiah fired his musket. Its lead ball thudded into the middle of the Tory's chest, and the man fell backward, his eyes wide with stunned surprise. Those eyes stayed open in death.

Now more Tories came charging down the hill, shooting their muskets and trying to quickly reload. Jeremiah had already reloaded and primed his musket, glad he'd practiced the routine to a quick perfection. He turned and fired at yet another uniformed Loyalist, then pressed against a tree as more lead balls crashed into that very tree trunk and sent bark flying. He thought what an ideal situation this was. The Tories were literally trapped at the top of the hill, surrounded by their enemy. They were forced to come down in their effort to move the enemy out of the way, and in doing so, they were easy targets.

He heard another crashing sound, and a string of cusswords. Peering around the tree trunk, he saw a uniformed soldier tumbling down the steep hill. Higgins howled with laughter at the sight, and when the soldier finally landed just a few feet from them, he scrambled to his feet and immediately put up his hands in a gesture of surrender. Higgins motioned for him to back up against the tree trunk.

"Don't shoot me!" the young man pleaded. His hat had come off, and he was covered with pine needles and dirt. Higgins laughed again and glanced at Jeremiah.

"Looks like we got us a prisoner."

"Looks like," Jeremiah answered. "Hey, Logan! Come take this one away!" He didn't know Higgins's comrade by any other name, wasn't even sure if Logan was a first or a last name. The buckskin-clad mountain man rose up from behind a cluster of smaller pine trees and came forward, waving his musket at the panicked Tory. "Over here," he ordered the soldier, looking eager to put a lead ball into the Englishman. "Send me some more!" he shouted to Jeremiah and Higgins as he poked his musket into the prisoner's back and led him behind the pine trees to a large rock formation, where he'd been ordered to wait on guard with other prisoners.

Now the gunfire came more rapidly, and from all directions. More Loyalist soldiers came charging down the hill, and several more of them fell. They were met by a barrage of gunfire from the mountain men and Continentals, and soon the air was filled with acrid smoke from gunpowder, and with war cries and the screams of the wounded. An English soldier charged Jeremiah with his bayonet, and Jeremiah jumped aside at the last minute, whirling with his hunting knife and ramming it into the soldier's back. The man screamed in agony, then collapsed.

From then on, and for the next several minutes, there was no time to wonder what happened to Higgins or Logan or any of the others. It was each man for himself. Jeremiah grunted when the point of a bayonet glanced across his left thigh. He turned and slammed his musket barrel across the side of a soldier's face. The man crashed to the ground and lay still, and Jeremiah quickly primed and reloaded his musket. Immediately, he fired it at still another soldier, opening a hole in the man's face.

The fighting continued off and on for several hours, until at last the gunfire ceased and everything became strangely quiet.

"Jeremiah?" Higgins shouted. The man came bounding toward him from farther up the hill.

"Right here," Jeremiah answered. "You okay?"

"So far," the man answered when he drew close. "You?"

"One sonofabitch cut my damn leg open." Jeremiah looked

down to see blood soaking his ripped deerskin leggings. "A Delaware woman made these just for me not long ago," he grumbled.

Higgins chuckled. "You could be bleedin' to death, and you're worried about the damn leggings. Must be a special woman."

Jeremiah grinned. "I guess you could say that."

"Some of them Injun' women can be right pleasin' in a man's bedroll, right?"

Jeremiah decided not to answer the question. He didn't want to get into a match of words over Indian women. "Looks like the Tories are regrouping," he said, changing the subject.

"They ain't got a chance. Goin' up top that hill was the dumbest thing Ferguson could have done, next to insultin' us mountain men." He turned toward the tree shroud in the distance. "You all right, Logan?"

Logan stood up and waved his musket. "Got me two more prisoners, all tied up nice and tidy!"

Again shots rang out from above them. Jeremiah began to feel light-headed and hurried over to where Logan sat with three hog-tied Loyalist soldiers, one of them bleeding heavily from a wound on his forehead.

"Tie off my leg with some of that cord, will you?" Jeremiah said to Logan. "I'm bleeding like a stuck pig!"

Logan hurriedly tied a piece of rawhide around Jeremiah's thigh above the wound as more Loyalists and Tories came charging down for another attack and an attempt at escape. Again there were gunshots, screams and shouts, cries of pain, the air becoming blue and stinging to the eyes and nose from powder smoke.

Jeremiah ran to rejoin the fighting, and it was then that he saw an obvious commander of the Tories, riding a white horse and blowing on his whistle wildly. Jeremiah had no doubt it was Major Patrick Ferguson himself. He took aim and fired. Ferguson started to fall, and before he hit the ground, his body jerked wildly as more musket balls plowed into his flesh.

Patriots and mountain men began howling with victorious cheers and staged a strong defense as the rest of the Tories tore down the "mountain," some on horseback, most on foot, more falling on their way down. Jeremiah paid no heed to his bleeding leg as the excitement of battle rallied his weakening condition. He reloaded as he ran toward several Tories coming down in a group. He shot and killed one, whacked another with his musket, then drew his knife and rammed it into the chest of yet another. Whirling, dodging bayonets and lead balls, stabbing, kicking, and fighting with his fists, he entered the all-out brawl for the next several minutes, until finally most of the shooting stopped and the surviving Tories were waving their arms and shouting their surrender.

Confusion prevailed for another half hour or so until more Tories, both the wounded and unwounded, were rounded up as prisoners. As the situation became more orderly, it was obvious that virtually every Tory and Loyalist who'd been entrenched on King's Mountain had been either killed or captured, their leader dead.

Higgins pulled a flask of whiskey from a pouch he wore on his wide belt and slugged down some of the drink, then handed the flask to Jeremiah. "We made the bastard eat his words, didn't we!" he exclaimed.

"That we did!" Jeremiah replied, taking a long swallow of the whiskey himself to allay the pain in his leg. For some reason, Annie's face flashed into his mind when he closed his eyes as he drank. It was a strangely stunning experience, as though she were trying to speak to him. He lost his smile, handing the flask back to Higgins and frowning, wondering why the vision had come to him so suddenly and so vividly.

For the next several minutes, he couldn't get Annie off his mind as he helped round up more Tories to herd them in a march to the Cowpens, where prisoners were held temporarily.

Annie. Was she all right? What was happening back at Willow Creek?

20

October 8, 1780
Ohio Valley

Annie felt as though she was in prison. She wanted to scream her way out of the darkness that held her captive. It was enough torture living with the agony of her father's and brother's deaths, and the loss of her baby; but she also had to live with blindness, knowing she might never see Luke's face again, or the faces of her unborn children. In fact, it would be better that she never had children at all. She wouldn't be able to keep up with her own personal household chores, let alone watch after a child. How would she cook and bake for Luke? How would she knit his sweaters and mend his clothes? How did she know she'd even be able to have more children? And how would her and Luke's short marriage survive this living hell, especially now that Luke intended to leave her to seek some kind of revenge? How did a man even find revenge? Would it really help for him to kill every Tory he found?

That would not change what had happened. He could never find the exact men who'd attacked their farm and robbed them of everything precious, including her own virtue and sight ...

and her baby. Now she knew why God had rid her of her child. She could never have been a proper mother.

Her head ached from the constant bumping and jostling of the open-bed wagon in which she rode with her mother and sister. There was little talking as a cold rain seemed to penetrate all of them to the bone. Each sat with her own sorrowful thoughts, her mother mourning a dead son and husband and the blindness of a daughter; Sally mourning the loss of a father and brother. It was impossible to determine who should comfort whom. She needed her mother and sister to be strong, needed their comfort, and they in turn needed the comfort of her own strength and support.

Would she ever know happiness again? Would any of the forty or so others who traveled with them know a normal life again? Just about everyone in this entourage for survival had lost loved ones and property. Other farms had been burned and ran-sacked. Friends and neighbors had also suffered, and now they all clung to each other and watched out for each other as they traveled through thick forest and along the edge of the Ohio north to Fort Harmar, where they hoped to find safety.

Was *anyplace* safe anymore? War raged in the East, where surely not one man could trust another. Now it had visited their peaceful little settlement clear out on the frontier. Both sides had again roused the various Iroquois tribes to their side, probably making promises to rid the Indian lands of settlers if the Indians would help them. None of those promises would be kept, and in the interim, too many settlers would die . . . some of them hor-ribly and slowly at the hands of maniacal warriors who reveled in torture.

She couldn't help wondering about Jeremiah, too. Would she ever see him again? Where had he gone? Was he even still alive? Maybe he'd been found and hung, or killed in some battle. Now she would have to wonder the same things about Luke. Once they reached Fort Harmar, he would leave. He'd already told her so. His only mission was to get her to safety first.

She huddled into the woolen blanket she kept wrapped around her head and shoulders. Water dripped from the hooded part and splashed onto her hands. The raindrops reminded her of the many tears she'd shed over the last many days. There were so many things to cry about that they all tumbled together in her heart and mind, making her feel ill. She wished Luke could ride with her in the wagon, keep his arms around her. She needed his strength, needed to feel the safety of his embrace. She loved him so, yet was not sure she could forgive him if he left her now, as he was so determined to do. "You'll have your mother and sister," he'd reminded her. "And there are plenty of settlers and armed men at Fort Harmar, even some Patriots. The Indians up around there trade at the fort and haven't been any trouble."

That's what they had thought about the Indians around Willow Creek, and look at what had happened. Still, part of her could understand Luke's need for action. He was a man, a brave and strong man who'd been horribly wronged; a hardworking man who'd had everything he'd worked for destroyed. He'd go crazy sitting around Fort Harmar waiting to see what would happen next. He had to go and do something about his loss, about the harm his wife had suffered, about the loss of his child. This was the only way a man like Luke could find any kind of true relief.

Men shouted to the horses and oxen that pulled what wagons they were able to salvage from the destruction, carrying their few remaining belongings. She heard the sound of a horse riding closer, heard Luke's voice.

"Are you all right under there?" he called out to her.

Annie removed the blanket, but she just stared into darkness. "I don't even know. I'm cold and I feel numb."

How many would die along the way from consumption? Her mother had already been coughing badly, and Annie sensed that the woman's sagging spirit was getting worse.

"How much farther?" Annie asked Luke.

"Only a couple of days," he shouted back. "Just pray we don't get attacked by Indians or Tories before we get there."

Annie pulled the blanket back over her head. Those weren't just Tories fighting for what they believed in. They were no better than outlaws, using loyalty to the king as an excuse to ransack and rape and steal. They were *worse* than the common enemy. They had left Luke a changed man.

"Luke? Are you still there?"

She felt the wagon come to a halt, heard men shouting to take a rest. The rain poured harder.

"Luke?"

"Yes, I'm still here," he answered, his voice close. She felt a gentle grip on her arm. "Climb down out of there. We'll sit out of the rain for a while." He grasped her hand and ordered her mother and sister out of the wagon also as Annie stood up. "Just lean over," he told her.

Annie obeyed, and Luke grasped her around the waist and lifted her over the side of the wagon as though she weighed nothing. Instead of setting her on her feet, he moved his arms around her waist and hugged her close, her feet off the ground.

Annie wept on his shoulder. "Luke. I'm so sorry."

"Quit saying that. There was absolutely nothing you could have done." She felt him tense up. "But there is something *I* can do, and I will." He kept her tight against him. "I'm sorry to leave you, Annie, but I have to do it. Tell me you understand."

His voice was close to her ear.

"It would be easier if I could see, Luke. I'm so terrified not being able to see!"

He reached under her hips and lifted her, carrying her she knew not where, except that when he set her down, she could tell the rain was not hitting her.

"Luke?"

He sat down beside her. "We're under a shelf rock. It's more comfortable than sitting under the wagon." He pulled her into his arms. "I'll come back, Annie. You know that."

"No, I *don't* know that, and neither do you! Jeremiah probably thought he'd come back soon, too, and he was gone for three years. He didn't plan on being imprisoned on a ship. We didn't plan on being attacked, Luke. No one knows what will happen to him, especially now."

Luke sighed. "Annie . . ."

She felt him shudder and heard him choke. He was quietly weeping.

"I have to do this, Annie," he said gruffly. "I have to go. I would never feel like a whole man again if I didn't."

She breathed deeply of his scent, wanting always to remember it. "Then go," she said softly. "And God go with you."

21

October 9, 1780
South Carolina

Jeremiah kept his horse at a slow walk, following behind ten of the over five hundred captured Loyalists. Estimates were that roughly one thousand Tories and Loyalists had been either killed, wounded, or captured. Major Ferguson was dead, and the Patriots, most of them mountain men, felt quite proud of themselves. For two days, they'd herded their captives toward the Cowpens.

Riding beside Jeremiah, Ralph Higgins again put a flask of whiskey to his lips and tipped it, letting out a gruff "Ahhhh" after taking a swig. "Nothin' like a lick of good whiskey to top off a damn good fight." He handed over the flask. "Care to imbibe?"

Jeremiah gave him a strained smile and reached for the flask, hoping a swallow of liquor would help ease the pain in his leg. The bleeding had finally stopped, but the cut muscle pained him fiercely. He slugged down some of the whiskey and handed back the flask.

"Where you goin' next?" Higgins asked.

"Don't know."

"Me, I'm headin' back to my mountain home in North Carolina. Got me a woman there."

Jeremiah thought about Annie, and Higgins's remark made him realize he really had no particular place to go now. He might as well head farther north and find out what else he could do to help end this war. The victory at King's Mountain surely helped the Patriot cause.

"You ain't goin' to see that there Injun' woman what made them leggin's for you?" Higgins asked.

Jeremiah smiled at the thought of Shara. "Her father is a friend. That's all there is to it. She's probably wed to some fancy warrior by now. Besides, the Patriot cause comes first."

"Patriot cause!" one of the prisoners ahead of them sneered. He turned to look back and spit at Jeremiah's horse. "You're all damned idiots if you think you can defeat the king's army. England owns half the world! What makes you think you have a chance against her?"

Jeremiah gave his horse a slight kick so that the animal lurched and nearly knocked the prisoner over. The man grabbed the horse's bridle to keep his balance and glared at Jeremiah, who took his foot from the stirrup and kicked the prisoner in the face, knocking the man to the ground. "That's what makes me think I have a chance," he growled at the man. "And with France on our side, it won't be long before England pulls out of the United States without so much as a last look!"

The prisoner, his nose bleeding profusely, managed to get up as Jeremiah circled him on horseback. Higgins laughed at the sight. The prisoner's dark uniform was ripped, and one boot was missing. The man limped forward, but Jeremiah rode around him again and cut him off, studying the young man, whose hair was a tangled mass of sandy curls. "You know anything about other Tory or Loyalist attacks?"

"You stinking Patriot! Why would I tell you if I did?" The man spoke with his hand over his nose, blood dripping through his fingers.

"Because I just might decide to pound that nose into pudding if you don't," Jeremiah answered, still riding circles around the man he figured roughly the same age as himself. He reined his horse in such a manner that the animal kept bumping into the prisoner. "Do you want any kind of nose left at all, or would you prefer to just have two holes in your face?"

"Bastard!" the man swore, bending over to let the blood flow more freely for a moment. "You're not a respectable soldier at all. You and your friend are just a couple of illiterate mountain men!"

Jeremiah turned his horse to bump the man sideways, making him fall again. "I assure you, mister, that I am quite literate. And right now I'm feeling a lot of pain from a Loyalist's bayonet, so I'm not in a very good mood. I've got other things on my mind that just put me in an even *worse* mood, so don't tempt me to make good on my threat."

Higgins laughed more, taking another swig of whiskey. "You tell him, Jeremiah!"

In the distance, some of the other prisoners were being harassed, all but a few of them forced to walk the long distance to the Cowpens, where prisoners from other, smaller skirmishes were already being held.

The prisoner stayed on the ground, rolling to a sitting position. He pulled up his shirttail and held it to his nose. "What the hell do you want from me?" he asked Jeremiah, sounding almost ready to cry.

Wincing with pain, Jeremiah dismounted, pulling his hunting knife from its sheath. "I want you to tell me what you know about other Tory movements." He stepped close and grasped hold of the man's thick curls, taking a fistful in his left hand and slashing the knife through them. The man cried out and cringed.

Jeremiah dropped the handful of hair in front of the prisoner. "I could easily have gone deeper, mister. I've fought *with* Indians, and *against* Indians, and I know of all kinds of ways to make a man talk. Would you like to know what some of them are?"

Still holding his shirttail to his nose, the man looked around as though thinking to get help.

"The rest of the prisoners and Patriots are heading on," Jeremiah reminded him. "Won't be long before it will be just you and me."

"What the hell do you *want?*" the prisoner repeated.

"You *know* what I want! I heard talk about plans to attack western settlements. Have any of those plans been carried out?"

The prisoner ran his free hand through his clipped hair. "Why do you think *I* know anything, mister?"

Jeremiah reached down and literally lifted the man to his feet by the hair of his head, making him cry out with more pain. He kept hold of his hair as he held his hunting knife to the man's bleeding nose while he spoke. "You know something, because earlier I saw you put a piece of paper in your mouth and *swallow* it! What was on that piece of paper you didn't want any of us to see?"

"I . . . nothing."

Jeremiah lowered the knife to the man's throat. "Do I need to rip your guts open and look for the paper *myself?*"

"You wouldn't!"

Jeremiah lowered the knife. "Don't bet on it!"

The prisoner swallowed. "Put the knife away, please. Put the knife away and I'll tell you."

Glaring at him, Jeremiah stepped back and slid the knife back into its sheath, never taking his eyes off the man.

"Well, well," Higgins muttered. "I never seen him eat that paper," he told Jeremiah. He remained on his horse, leaning forward in anticipation. "What *was* on that paper, mister?"

Closing his eyes for a moment, the man kept the shirt to his nose. "It was just a list."

Jeremiah frowned. "A list? Of what?"

"Something I was using to keep track of where I knew other companies of Tories would strike. I was at a meeting a few weeks ago where lots of plans were made."

"Is that so?" Jeremiah folded his arms. "And just where are these strikes intended to take place?"

The man shrugged. "I swallowed the list. I can't remember all of them. I know some of us are headed for Charleston, some to Savannah, some up toward Yorktown, all the places you'd expect, I suppose. The English troops need our help on all fronts."

"Of course they do. They're fighting a losing battle."

"I happen to disagree." The man wiped at his nose and squinted his eyes with pain as he studied Jeremiah. "Loyalists and Tories have already taken strongholds along the frontier," he added. "We decided it was important to make sure the Patriots were cleared out from the Ohio Valley east so that all areas were covered."

Jeremiah frowned. "The Ohio Valley? Isn't that pretty remote for the Tories to be worrying about it?"

The man managed a haughty grin, but his nose literally sat crooked on his face, and a dark swelling was beginning to show around it. Jeremiah also noticed a tooth missing where the man's upper lip was cut.

"That, sir, is how you win wars. You make sure the enemy isn't congregating in unexpected places. While England, with our help, wins the war here in the populated areas, some of us are making sure more rebels aren't meeting in the remote areas and planning further trouble, let alone gathering additional men to their side. And, of course, there could be Patriots hiding in those areas."

The mention of the Ohio Valley alarmed Jeremiah. Were Luke and Annie in danger? "How would you know who was a Loyalist and who was a Patriot in such areas?"

The man raised his chin, looking ridiculous in his torn clothes, a large notch of hair missing from his thick curls, his nose crooked and purple, his lip cut and a tooth missing. Jeremiah wanted to laugh, taking great pleasure in being able to vent his anger on the enemy. But for the moment, laughter was out of the question.

"We have our spies," the man answered.

Jeremiah glowered at him, more worried now. "Name some of them."

The man shook his head, putting his shirt to his nose again. "I would if I could. I really don't know. I am only familiar with the men I was with on King's Mountain. I heard several names, but there is no way I could remember them all."

Jeremiah again pulled out his knife. "Were they on that list?"

The man paled visibly, losing his confidence as he looked Jeremiah over. "No. Just places, not names."

Jeremiah stepped closer, hiding the pain in his thigh. "Well, how about naming some of the places?"

The man glanced at Jeremiah's knife, then sighed. "A place

called Briscoe's Settlement, Musk Bottom, or something like that."

"Muskingum Bottom?"

"Maybe. Something like that."

Briscoe's Settlement was too damned close to Willow Creek. Jeremiah's heart pounded harder.

"What about Willow Creek? Did you hear that name?"

The man nodded. "Sounds familiar. And a place called Fort Harmar."

Jeremiah shoved his knife into its sheath again. "Were the attacks planned for the future, or do you think they have already taken place?"

The prisoner shook his head. "Hard to say. Some have probably already taken place."

"Jesus," Jeremiah muttered under his breath. He turned to Higgins. "It's been nice knowing you, Higgins. Maybe we'll meet again. Meantime, take care of this man. I'm leaving."

"*Leaving?* Where to?"

"I've got family at Willow Creek. I've got to go there and see if they're all right." Jeremiah grunted as he managed to re-mount his horse.

"Can't you wait and leave in the morning?" Higgins asked.

Jeremiah shook his head. "I can't get there any too soon!" Without another word, he kicked his horse into a gallop and headed west. It would take up to three weeks to reach Willow Creek. Anything could happen by then. Anything!

"*Annie!*"

He should have gone back after he healed. What if he'd failed her yet again? And Luke! His brother might need him to help protect the farm. Much as he hated the thought of having to be around Annie again, he felt obligated to warn Luke and to stay there and help keep watch for a while. Luke had worked his hind end off on that farm for years. He didn't deserve to lose it . . . or to lose Annie.

22

October 15, 1780
Fort Harmar, Ohio Valley

Gone! Luke was gone. Annie had never felt more alone, trapped here at Fort Harmar, a blind person in unfamiliar surroundings. Wherever she went, her mother or sister had to lead her. The weather was shivering damp, rain combining with the chill to make her feel the dankness right to the bone. The cabin outside the fort walls, where she and what was left of her family lived with two widowed women, never seemed warm enough. She could only hope the warm weather that sometimes returned at this time of year would make another appearance, giving the few men here time to chop and stow up enough wood to get them all through what could be a very long, hungry winter.

Annie lay on the drafty floor of the cabin, huddled into several quilts and trying to make sense of her life. The shocking changes of the past two weeks left her numb. The house was gone—and Luke's beautiful farm—and worse, the baby she'd been so excited to tell Luke about. On top of all that, her father was dead . . . and young Calvin. Poor Calvin.

And poor Luke, a proud man, a man of peace. He'd been

pushed too far. Sure she was safe here, he'd bid her good-bye, and even though she couldn't see him, she could sense the change in him. She'd felt his anger, and she knew that the gentleness in his blue eyes was surely gone now, replaced by a fierce desire for revenge.

How lonely he must be now. She wanted to be with him. What if he was wounded? She should be there to comfort him. Luke and several other men had left together, planning first to visit John Hagan. Annie shuddered to think of what would happen to the man, if indeed he'd not already fled Willow Creek. Others had heard his name, and all had no doubt that Hagan was a spy and responsible for the raid on the town and outlying farms. Those who'd made it here had horrific tales to tell of hideous tortures at the hands of the Wyandots, the tribe that took part in the raids. That gave Annie only one thing to be glad about . . . that she and Luke had not suffered the same hideous death. Their lives had been spared, but for what, she could not imagine, for now Luke was gone and possibly might never return . . . and she was left sightless.

She managed to take hope in the fact that the blackness of her world seemed to be fading somewhat to more of a brown haze. Many were praying that her sight would gradually return, but after all that had transpired in her life over the past several days, Annie had trouble believing there was a God in heaven who listened to anything a person prayed for. Her mother was a broken woman, having lost a son and a husband to awful deaths, another son missing, her oldest daughter blinded, uprooted from her home.

Nearly every person here had terrible tales of loss—loss of property, of loved ones, of innocent and unarmed people. The attacks were acts of pure murder. Luke had agreed, and now many of those grieving and unarmed people were armed and ready to return the killing and mayhem. Where would it all end?

"Annie!"

Annie felt someone shaking her and recognized her mother's voice.

"Get up! We have to head inside the fort!"

"Why?"

"Scouts say there are Shawnee coming!"

"My God!" Annie moaned. How much more could she and the others here suffer? She quickly rose, keeping a quilt wrapped around her. Her mother helped her slip her stockinged feet into a pair of leather boots that had belonged to young Calvin. They were a little big on her, but they came to her knees and would be good protection in deeper snows, or if she had to run through thick brush to escape an attack. It would be a few weeks before snow would be a worry, but God only knew how long they would all be huddled into Fort Harmar for survival. And if she lost her mother, how could she run from the enemy when she couldn't see?

"Let's go!" Ethel took her daughter's arm, and Annie felt Sally grasp her other arm. She sensed her little sister's terror.

"We'll be all right, Sally," she lied, hoping to ease the girl's fears.

Together they exited the cabin and started running. Annie had to trust her mother and sister to lead her in a way that would keep her from stumbling over something. It was only a matter of a couple hundred yards to the walled fort, but in times like these, that could seem like two miles. Annie felt her heart pounding, and she wondered how much longer she could live this way.

Run! Run! Run! She kept the quilt draped around her shoulders, felt the rain pouring down on her head and face. Such a cold rain. Now she could hear shouting, men giving orders to take cover and "wait for your best shot!" That would be Hugh Clay giving the orders. He was a take-charge character who'd seemed to just naturally take command after most of the other men left. Clint Thom was here, too, and his son Billy.

Fort Harmar wasn't a true fort in the sense that it sheltered real soldiers. It was simply a place for settlers to run to when an Indian attack was imminent, and apparently that was the case now. Annie had hoped that the attacks were over and the Tories would move on, but everyone's greatest fears were being realized. Knowing that the area settlers were weakened and fewer in number, the Shawnee most likely had decided this might be a good time to chase out *all* pilgrims from what the Indians considered their territory. Why not finish what the Tories started?

Now she heard more men, children crying, shouted orders. She could hear the scrape of rods being pounded into muskets to pack the black powder, heard a horse ride past them, heard someone shout at them to "Hurry!" Moments later, she sensed they were inside the fort's perimeter.

"Close the doors!" someone commanded.

Already, Annie heard gunfire. Her mother and sister kept running with her, taking her inside what she knew was a stronghold that had only small openings through which a man could aim his musket. Now she knew she was huddling down with countless other women and children, while outside, the firing gradually intensified until within a few minutes, it seemed almost constant.

Annie waited in her mother's arms, wanting to cover her ears when, after a while, they could hear the war cries and screams of the invading Shawnee. The sounds made her feel ill as she remembered the same sounds when she and Luke were attacked.

"There are too many of them!" a man inside the stronghold shouted. "My God! They're swarming the walls!"

The shouts came closer. Men cried out, terrible screams of agony. Annie suspected they were falling under the blows of hatchets. What else were the Indians doing to them? At the moment, she was almost glad she couldn't see. Some of the women began to cry. Children whimpered. Men inside the stronghold began firing frantically, ordering women nearby to load spare muskets as fast as they could. Before long, something began pounding at the doors, and Ethel's grip on Annie's arm tightened. Her mother began praying, and Sally rested her head against Annie's shoulder and started to cry.

Annie drew on a deep determination not to cry. She'd done enough of that. If she was meant to die on this day, then she would die. Her only prayer was that it would happen quickly. She moved her arms around her mother and sister. "I love you both," she told them.

"I love you, too," Sally answered, shaking.

"God be with us," Ethel said softly, kissing Annie's cheek.

In the next moment, the doors burst open. Blood-chilling war cries filled the room, women and children screamed, men shouted. Shots were fired, and then Annie could hear the sickening sound of hatchets splitting skulls, bayonets scraping into bodies. She could literally smell the blood.

Suddenly, she felt her mother ripped away from her. "Annie!" Ethel screamed.

"Mama," Annie groaned, saying a quick prayer that her mother would die quickly.

Next came twelve-year-old Sally, who also screamed Annie's name. Her screams continued and then began to fade. Annie strained to hear amid the horrible shouting and screaming and thuds of hatchets. She sensed that Sally was being carried away rather than killed. Would her fate be even worse than death? Poor Sally!

She waited for her own death blow. Gradually, the screams of those who'd been huddled with her began to die out, and there was only the noise of the Indians' war cries and more chopping, thudding sounds. They were hacking up the dead! She waited for a blade to sink into her back. Why was she still alive?

23

October 10, 1780
Pennsylvania

Luke trudged through the lowland along the Susquehanna River as he and those with whom he traveled headed for Philadelphia. They'd heard it was there that they could discover the latest happenings in the revolution and find out how they might best be used. He led his horse, the animal weary and almost useless from the long trip. It was one of only two of his horses left after the raid, and certainly not one of his best. The aging roan mare was barely up to the journey that had brought them here, and Luke did not doubt that he'd soon be walking everyplace he went, unless the Continental Army could provide him with a horse, which was doubtful.

So far, the talk was that the United States government was as close to broke as any assemblage could be without declaring bankruptcy. He highly doubted that good horses would be available, let alone any of the meager pay those who joined up would receive. Still, he and those with him cared little at the moment about compensation. The real purpose of being here was to rid America of English rule and of the Tories and Loyalists who'd exacted heavy tolls on innocent people who simply happened to disagree with them.

Never in his life had he felt such bitterness and hatred. All those years he'd spent working his farm, cutting trees, pulling stumps, toiling at building his future . . . all that was for nothing, since that's what was left for him. Nothing. There was no house, no barn, no livestock, no crops . . . and now no baby. His beautiful new wife was blind and filled with grief and despair. His own nature had turned from joyful and hopeful to thirsting for revenge.

He'd satisfied part of that thirst when he and those with him attacked John Hagan's farm. Before this, killing another human being, other than rapacious Indians, would have haunted him and filled him with remorse. He felt none of that now. He'd dealt one of the many blows under which Hagan had fallen in the brutal beating he'd suffered at the hands of angry settlers. He'd helped put the torch to Hagan's home and outbuildings. It felt good to destroy the man! He hadn't even felt anything at the sight of Hagan's wife screaming and weeping. He had no idea what the woman had done after they left. She didn't dare go to Fort Harmar. The Hagan children were grown and gone, having departed to fight with the Tories, something Luke and the others had never known. All this time, they'd thought Hagan's sons were fighting as Patriots. But now the time had come when no man could trust the other; now he realized why Jeremiah had been so passionate about his war.

Annie! Every time he thought about the woman with whom he'd shared his bed with such sweet satisfaction, he ached for her. At least she was safe. The Tories and Shawnee had surely moved on to other areas. His only prayer now was that Annie would recover her eyesight. Just before he left, she'd told him that things seemed a little lighter. Surely, God had allowed enough destruction and heartache. Surely, Annie would at least be allowed to see again.

It made him feel sick to think of the helplessness he'd experienced the day of the attack, knowing those men were raping her. *Raping* her! And it was the *white* men who'd done it, not the Indians! *Bastards!* He couldn't kill enough Tories for that. He couldn't kill enough English soldiers for that. This was the only way he could vent his frustrations and somehow make up for not being able to protect her. God, how he loved her! He'd loved her for years . . . waited for her for years. Finally sharing his bed with her had been pure ecstasy, at last being able to be one with her, to give her everything that once was only his . . . but now, all he'd given her was gone, not just his home and property, but even the special sexual gift they'd shared. God knew if she would ever want to lie with him again after what those men did. Maybe she even blamed him for it, for living so far from help. He should have sent her to town when whispers of possible attacks began. At least at Willow Creek, with others around, she might have been spared the horrors of a sexual attack.

"You think that George Washington, or maybe even your brother, will be in Philadelphia?"

Preacher Falls asked the question. Even a man of the cloth had joined them in the fight. He'd not taken part in the beating death of John Hagan, but he'd helped burn the man's farm, then actually prayed afterward with the rest of them for help in fighting for independence, while in the background, Margaret Hagan wept uncontrollably over her husband's beaten, bloodied body.

"Who knows?" Luke answered. The two men followed a well-worn road toward their destination. "They both could be anyplace. I'll just have to ask around about Jeremiah when we meet up with other soldiers."

"Do you really think the new government is broke?"

"Wouldn't surprise me. Maybe France will bail us out."

"He who was once an enemy is now a friend."

Luke managed a grin. "Bible?"

Preacher Falls smiled, too, shaking his head. "No. Me."

Luke sighed. "War certainly changes a man's outlook, doesn't it?"

"Certainly does. I'm not sure I'm still fit to preach about love and peace."

"You are. You still believe in those things. But doesn't the Bible refer to avenging angels at times?"

"Well, there's the key word. *Angels.* Not men. I hardly consider any of us angels."

Luke sobered. "Annie is."

. "I'm sure she's close, Luke."

"Do you think God will let her see again?"

"None of us can know His will. And don't forget there is another force at work in times like these. We can't let that force destroy our trust in God."

Luke watched the road ahead, able now to see the outline of a large settlement. *Must be Philadelphia.* Were they here already? He remembered that several weeks after the first new Congress of the United States met here, messengers had brought the news to the frontier settlements. At that time, cities like Philadelphia seemed unreal, faraway places he never even cared to see. He'd long forgotten what Albany had been like, he'd been so small when he left there with Jeremiah. He'd lived in remote Willow Creek for so long that it seemed incredible to be back in true "civilization" again.

Maybe he and Annie should move here when all this was over, someplace where there were lots of people, and Indians were no longer a threat. He felt burdened by the constant worry of attack. It hadn't mattered so much when he was single, but everything had changed. The realization of how quickly and brutally he could lose Annie burned in his gut. Leaving her at Fort Harmar was the hardest thing he'd ever done, but at least she had her mother and sister, and she was protected. For now, he could only hope she still loved him when he returned, and somehow he'd find a way to pick up the pieces of their lives and put them back together.

24

Late October, 1780

Annie forced all feelings, including fear, to shut down. She refused terror, refused anguish, refused sorrow. She refused to feel any pain, either physical or emotional. For now, survival was the key word. Why she'd been spared, she could not imagine. She'd sat at the fort, blind and waiting for the hatchet to fall. It never did. Instead, she was grabbed by two men, and she didn't have to see to know they were Shawnee.

She was now their prisoner. She'd been led to a horse, lifted onto it. One of the men had mounted up behind her, and amid the smell of blood and the agonizing groans of those settlers still alive, they rode off. She had no idea where she was being taken, or why. Was it to be slave to some warrior, or slave to his wives? Would she be slowly tortured to death? She'd heard some of the lurid details of ways the Shawnee had of bringing exquisite pain to their captives, who died slowly and horribly.

To her best guess, they had been riding for nearly two weeks, and during that time, she'd begun to see light, enough to know if it was day or night. She had not been physically abused, starved, or forbidden water, and at night, she was given blankets to keep her warm. God only knew how she looked by now, but that didn't matter. Her gentle treatment confused her, especially after the awful massacre at Fort Harmar.

Today they made camp in what seemed to be a grassy, sunny place, and she sensed they had joined up with others of their kind. The warm sun on her face told her the weather had brought one of those beautiful, blue-sky days often experienced at this time of year, "the last days of summer," her mother used to call them.

She prayed that her beloved mother had died quickly. The thought of Ethel Barnes being gone from her life brought a fierce ache to her chest and she longed to cry, but that was another feeling she refused to allow. All of that would have to wait until she was rescued . . . if indeed that ever happened. Surely, when Luke returned, he would see what had happened at Fort Harmar. He would begin looking for her, and perhaps, by some miracle, he would be able to find her. That was most likely an impossibility, but she knew she had to cling to that hope, and to pray Luke wouldn't think her already dead and not try searching at all.

She heard men talking, their voices slightly raised in what sounded like perhaps some kind of greeting. Then she heard a new voice, a laugh. Had someone else joined them? She smelled the smoke of campfires, and someone came close then and spoke to her in the Indian tongue she'd heard so much of lately. He shoved a piece of something warm and greasy into her hand. She smelled it, and it seemed to be some kind of meat. It mattered little what it was, only that it was food and she'd better eat it. She bit into it, surprised at how good it tasted. And as always, she simply sat there and waited for whatever might happen next.

The men's voices she'd heard minutes earlier now came closer, the Indians talking excitedly. A shadow came across the light in front of her eyes. "What's your name, woman?" a man asked.

Annie took hope. "You're white?"

"I'm a long hunter and a trader, and sometimes I work for the English, mapping out new lands for settlement. I know the Shawnee tongue."

"Is that who has me? The Shawnee?" Annie smelled old leather, perspiration, the odor of a man who lived most of his life outdoors and seldom bathed.

"Yes, ma'am. They're takin' you to Piqua Town, along the Mad River. Now, tell me your name."

"Annie. Annie Barnes—I mean, Annie Wilde. I hadn't been married long when I was taken. I'm still getting used to using my married name." She wiped grease from her hands onto her skirt. *My married name. Luke! Please come back!* "Why are they taking me to Piqua Town?"

"Somethin' to do with you bein' blind. They think you have special powers or somethin'."

So, she just might not be tortured and killed after all . . . or perhaps they thought an especially horrible torture was in order, to gain "possession" of her "spiritual" powers. She'd heard that some Indians thought they could take on the strength and spirituality of a captive by tasting his or her blood as they were tortured to death.

"I have no special powers. Surely you know that's just an Indian superstition. Can you convince them to let me go? Are you friends with them?"

"Somewhat. I came here to barter with them on some land, and they told me about you, wanted me to tell you not to be afraid. They won't hurt you."

The man's voice was gruff, but Annie sensed a hint of concern. "Tell them I'm not afraid and never have been. I am too proud for that, and I am very angry with them for what they did to my friends and my mother at Fort Harmar."

The trader said something in the Indian tongue, and several of the warriors laughed. Annie reached out, touching the deerskin jacket of the trader. "What is your name? Can you help me?"

"Name's Boone. Daniel Boone. Don't know if I can help. Once the Shawnee make up their minds they want to keep a captive, there's not much a man can do about it without losing his scalp . . . or sufferin' somethin' worse. I'm one man, and there must be forty or so warriors here. You can understand."

Annie nodded, sensing a goodness behind the rather wild ruggedness this Daniel Boone emitted. "Of course. Tell me, do you know a long hunter by the name of Jeremiah Wilde?"

"Jeremiah? Sure, I've met him. We're not exactly best friends, but I know him."

Annie took great hope in the revelation. "He's my brother-in-law," she told Boone. "I'm married to Luke Wilde. Could you please, when you leave here, do your best to find one of them? They're both off helping with the war. I don't know whose side you are on, but they are Patriots. I beg you not to hold that against them if you are a Loyalist. Just please, please, do what you can to find them and let them know where I will be. They will be so worried when they find out what happened at Willow Creek and Fort Harmar."

"I'll do my best, ma'am. That's as far as I can go, considerin' you'll be holed up in the middle of the Shawnee Nation. I'm not sure either of the Wilde brothers can do anything either."

"Jeremiah would find a way," Annie told him confidently, her heart suddenly filling with renewed feelings for Jeremiah, that strange admiration she had for his wilder side. "I know he'll try, if he knows where I am."

"I don't see a way out of this for you, Mrs. Wilde. I'll do some talking myself with the leader here. He's called Cornstalk, and it's a wise man who chooses not to cross him. Once I leave here, I'll spread the word where you are."

"Thank you. That gives me some hope."

"How is it you're blind?"

She shivered at the painful memory. "Tories attacked my husband's farm back at Willow Creek, destroyed everything. They"—she closed her eyes—"abused me and beat me. They also beat my husband. It was a blow to the back of my head that caused the blindness, I believe, and now I'm beginning to see light. I'm hoping the sight will return."

"Could very well happen, ma'am. Must be a terrifying way to live, not knowing where you are or what will happen to you, unable to see your captors or the land around you."

"It is, but I'm trying to be strong. Luke or Jeremiah will find me. I know they will."

"Well, I hope you're right, ma'am." He took her hand and squeezed it, and Annie sensed him rising. The shadow in front and to her left, and she could hear Daniel Boone talking with more Shawnee as their voices began to fade. She thought how odd it would feel, if indeed the man ended up helping her, to not even know what he looked like, and probably never to meet him again. Perhaps he was simply an angel sent by God to calm her . . . and to answer her prayers for freedom from this hell.

25

Jeremiah neared Willow Creek, the memory of Luke's ravaged farm burning in his soul, and his hatred for Tories at its peak. The new barn, the beautiful house—gone! Crops and wagons burned! Frozen carcasses of dead animals lying scattered. What he'd found at the farm brought horrifying imaginings of what could have happened to his brother . . . and to the woman they both loved.

Luke! Annie! Were they alive? He hardly knew for whom to mourn the most. He loved them both in such different ways. Was all of this his fault, for having gone to Willow Creek in the first place? Had some spy told on him? Who the hell could a man trust anymore?

His horse lathered, he approached the outskirts of what once was a peaceful, thriving settlement. Already he could see there was nothing left of it now. Trading stores were burned to the ground, as was the little log church where Luke had made Annie his wife. His heart pounded with dread. How could either of them still be alive after what he'd found at the farm, and now here? He slowed his horse to a walk as he rode through town toward Annie's old home.

It was still there, but the wooden fence made of tree branches that Henry had built around the front of the house was totally broken down. The door stood open, and even from here, he could see that the inside was ransacked. The only family he'd known for most of his growing-up years could all be dead. He should have stayed. Maybe he could have helped. But no. He'd had to leave, out of his own thirst for more war and fighting. He hated himself for it . . . yet how could he have stayed on here, having to see Annie with his brother . . . watching her . . . wanting her. It would have been too hard for both of them, and unfair to Luke.

It was then he noticed smoke in the distance, a trailing wisp of it that told him it came from a campfire. Indians? Trappers? Tories? It could be anyone, friend or foe. He dismounted, leading his horse farther before tying the animal for a much-needed rest and going on by foot. He kept his musket in hand, loaded and ready to shoot, as always. A fresh snow muffled his steps, and his breath showed in quick puffs of steam as it hit the cold air.

Cautiously, he approached the area from where he'd spotted the smoke rising, and he heard men's voices. As he stealthily crept closer, he also heard a woman's voice. It sounded shaky and full of sorrow. He peered through pine branches to see a gray-haired woman bent over an open fire, stirring something in an iron pot hanging from a tripod. A flatbed wagon nearby was stained black in places, apparently from sitting too close to a much larger fire, perhaps a remnant rescued from the ruins of town.

Four men sat nearby on logs, one of them bearded and shaking his head. Another had cloth bandages wrapped around his head, and Jeremiah could see bloodstains on it. All four men wore clothes that looked dirty and tattered.

"We might as well stay," one of them said. "It's less likely than ever now that they will come back. Pete here—" the man indicated the one with the bandaged head "—figures they've probably gone on north now with their loot, or they'll head back south by another way so they can do more raiding on their way. That there Boone fella' claims they'll just lay low at Piqua Town for the winter."

"Poor Annie," the one called Pete said, still shaking his bandaged head. "Wish I could have stopped them, but what the hell could I do? There were so many of them. So many. I can't believe any of us is still alive."

Jeremiah recognized the one with the injured head as Pete Shoenig, owner of a trading store in Willow Creek. Another was David Streffling, who'd had a farm not far from Luke's. His wife Jane used to bake cookies for Jeremiah and Luke, and she was the one who now stirred the food, but there seemed to be no life in her movements. The other two men sitting in the sad-looking group were farmers, Carl Bonner and Cole Jasper.

Pete's mention of the name Annie brought Jeremiah fully alert, and he hurried forward through the trees. Shoenig knew something about Annie!

All four men at the campfire quickly rose and reached for their muskets as Jeremiah approached.

"It's all right," Jeremiah called out. "It's me. Jeremiah Wilde. You all know me."

"Jeremiah!" Carl Bonner, a middle-aged man whose face showed the tanned wrinkles of years of hard work under the sun, set his musket aside. "You're alive! We wasn't sure after the Redcoats took you away with them last summer." The man stepped forward and put out his hand. "The way things have been, it's good to see *some*body still alive!"

Jeremiah shook his hand. "From what I've seen back at Willow Creek, I feel the same. I heard from captured Tories back in South Carolina about a month ago that attacks were planned for this area. All I could think about was my brother. I had to come and see if everyone was all right." He left the man, turning to Pete Shoenig, who had sat back down on the log. "Pete, I heard you mention Annie. Were you talking about Luke's wife? What's happened here? What do you know about Annie?"

Pete, his hair whiter than Jeremiah remembered, looked up at him with a sorrowful gaze. "You don't want to know, Jeremiah."

Jeremiah frowned, bending down to face the man. "I sure as hell do. Tell me, Pete." His stomach lurched at the thought of all the possibilities.

Pete sighed. "As you can see, Tories raided Luke's farm and most of the others around here, then paid a visit to Willow Creek."

"There was a real organized mob of them, Jeremiah," Cole Jasper put in. "It was awful, some of the things they did. Killed a whole lot of people, raped women, stole livestock. It was the worst thing I've ever seen. They was helped by Indians, mostly Wyandot, I think, some Mingo and Shawnee."

Jeremiah continued watching Pete, feeling sorry for the devastation in the man's eyes. "Those of us who survived headed for Fort Harmar for protection, including your brother and Annie. Her pa and younger brother were killed at Willow Creek. Her ma and sister went along to the fort."

Jeremiah rose and turned away. "What else?" He watched Jane Streffling continue stirring the contents of the black pot, staring at it as though not even aware of what she was doing. Tears trickled down her aged, wrinkled cheeks.

"Well, it's bad enough that in the attack on Luke's farm, Luke was beat near to death, and Annie was . . . raped," Pete continued.

Fury surged through Jeremiah like hot fire. "Jesus," he murmured.

"Probably worse than that was, the attack on Annie caused her to lose a baby . . . and left her blind," Pete added, his words coming slowly and with agonizing labor.

Jeremiah stepped away, his head suddenly aching from fierce feelings of guilt and anger. *Annie! My God, Annie!* And what had this done to poor Luke?

"Once Luke got Annie settled in at Fort Harmar—all of us went there, by the way," Carl told Jeremiah—". . . Luke, he figured Annie and her ma and sister was safe . . . figured the attacks were over. He was so full of rage that he left, went looking for you and looking for revenge. We found out it was John Hagan who helped set up the raids. Luke and a bunch of them left to kill Hagan and sack his farm. Then Luke and most of them went on to join up with the Patriots."

Jeremiah shook his head, all the news almost too much to comprehend. "Luke left Annie, when she was blind and suffering?" He turned to face Pete. "She must be terrified!"

"You didn't see him, Jeremiah. A man gets that much rage in him, he's got to do something about it. He made sure first that Annie was safe, and he vowed to come back. He figured she had her ma and sister to look after her."

"You say that like there's more to tell me."

The man rubbed at his head wound. "There is. After Luke left, Shawnee came along and attacked the fort. Killed most of the folks there. We're pretty much the only survivors, except for Annie and Sally. Their ma was killed, hacked up into nothing. Sally was carried off, and they took Annie, too. Strange thing was, they never laid a hand on her. They led her to a horse and put her on it and rode off, but they looked at her like she was something special, like maybe they were fascinated by her being blind."

A tiny light of hope began to burn in Jeremiah's heart. "She's still alive?"

"Her and her sister both, far as we know," Carl told him. "We don't really know about Sally, but a couple days ago, a scout by the name of Daniel Boone came through here. Come to find out he'd come from a big camp of Shawnee, said he'd seen a white woman there by the name of Annie Wilde. Said she was bein' treated good. He talked to her and she told him her name and said to look for you and Luke to come help her. Boone said he knows you, said if you came here, to be sure to let you know about Annie. He said there's a whole village of Shawnee where she is, that they were headed for Piqua Town, where there will be hundreds more. He said he wanted to help her, but it was impossible for one man."

"Those poor girls," Jane said, weeping quietly. "And all of us who've worked so hard out here to build what we had." She kept shaking her head.

Jeremiah felt a mixture of sorrow and joy. Annie was alive, but a Shawnee captive. "One man or not, I'm going after Annie!" he told them.

"Boone made it sound like there's no way to get her out of there," Cole told him.

"I'll damn well find a way! I owe it to my brother!" Jeremiah turned to Pete again. "Boone didn't see Sally?"

Pete shook his head. "No, sir."

Jeremiah rose and paced. *Damn them!* No wonder Luke had left to fight. He could just imagine what his brother must be suffering, but still . . . poor Annie! What a horror. Luke would be even more devastated and riddled with guilt when he learned what happened at Fort Harmar. He faced Pete again. "What will all of you do now?"

Pete shrugged. "Stay on, I guess. Maybe when the war is over, the new government will send help out here."

"The English treatied with the Shawnee and other tribes in sixty-three, promising them the colonists wouldn't settle west of the Appalachians," Streffling added. "We all knew what to expect when coming here."

Cole Jasper nodded. His baggy eyes and balding head showed a man hard-worn by life on the frontier. "My wife died in childbirth a couple of years ago, bled to death, no help. My two sons were killed in the raid. I've got nothing left now, except a vow that the Indians and Tories won't win."

He looked up at Jeremiah, a burning determination in his bloodshot eyes.

"And I won't let anybody chase me back. The land here is better than anything back East. It's a farmer's heaven, and beautiful. The Ohio Valley has been home since I moved here with the wife and family eight years ago. They died helping me build on free land that would have belonged to my sons and their sons. I can't go back now. My family is buried here, and I'm staying here with them. I'll find me a new wife and build a new farm. So will everybody else here."

Jeremiah realized that Luke must feel the same way. He was the reason Luke had come here in the first place. He was the one who'd told his brother about the free land ripe for farming and how beautiful this country was. He'd loved it, too, but then he'd left to wander, while Luke built his life here. Now most of what he'd built was gone . . . except for Annie.

He had no choice but to do all he could to find her. She needed him now more than ever. It was his duty to rescue and take care of his brother's wife . . . until Luke returned . . . *if* he returned. If not, he would take care of Annie for the rest of her life. And for now, the war would have to wait.

26

November 15, 1780
Piqua Town, Western Ohio

"Annie! Annie!"

Annie stood up, now able to see shadows within the light, movement of people, and trees blowing in the wind. Her heart pounded at the sound of her little sister's voice. "Sally?"

"Annie!" Suddenly the girl was wrapping her arms around Annie's waist, sobbing uncontrollably.

"Sally! Oh, my God!" Annie hugged her sister tightly. "You're alive! Sally!" She kissed her sister's hair and began to cry. It was the first time she'd wept since being captured. "Where did you come from? What happened to you? Are you hurt? Have they done anything terrible to you?"

"No." Sally continued sobbing as she spoke. "Oh, Annie, you couldn't see! You couldn't see what they did to Mama! They chopped her up! They chopped her all up! Mama!"

Annie closed her eyes and just held her, both of them crumpling down to sit in the snow. Annie had been stripped by Shawnee women and clothed in a fur-lined tunic, fur moccasins, and a hooded jacket of beaver skins. A Shawnee woman who spoke a little English managed to explain to her what she was wearing, also explaining that she was "very special" and that the women were given orders to take good care of her and to ask about her dreams. Annie had no idea of what to tell them, so she'd lied and said that in her dreams, the Shawnee walked away from the Ohio Valley, heading west. She'd hoped that would convince them they should do just that. So far, she'd heard no reaction to her dreams, and she worried that her predictions were beginning to anger them, especially Cornstalk.

By Sally's heavy clothing, Annie could tell that her sister had also been well cared for.

"I'm not hurt," Sally told her, shivering with lingering sobs. "I thought they would chop me up, too, but they just took me someplace where there were other girls my age. They made me put on Indian clothes and gave me food to eat and started showing me how they make clothes and things."

Annie kept her sister wrapped in her arms as the girl positioned herself between Annie's legs, her back against Annie. Annie kissed her cheek. "I'm so glad you're alive, Sally. They are probably saving you to be a wife someday, but we'll run away first. We'll find a way. I promise." She hugged her tightly again, taking renewed hope in finding her beautiful little sister alive. In the bright sunshine, she could even catch the carroty-red color of Sally's hair. Her sight seemed to be improving every day, just like Luke had hoped it would.

Luke. Where was Luke? How in God's name would he ever find her? Was he even alive? Would she ever see him again? She wished she would wake up from this nightmare and find herself lying in bed next to him, feeling him hold her . . . making love to her, taking away all the horror. Somehow, they would find each other again, find the sweet love they had shared.

"What made them bring you here, Sally?" she asked.

"I don't know. A man came to our camp, a white man. He was called Daniel Boone. I heard him telling somebody about you, and I yelled out that you were my sister. He said the Shawnee consider you special, and that maybe if they knew I was your sister, they would bring me to you. He told them in their language, and he was right. They did bring me!" She pressed her back even tighter against Annie. "Oh, Annie, I wanted to die! When I heard you were alive, I was so happy! Now I don't want to die anymore."

"And you won't. Neither of us will, Sally. We'll find a way out of this. I told Mr. Boone to look everywhere for Luke and Jeremiah. Maybe he will find one of them, or both, and they will come for us. Daniel Boone is telling everyone he meets that he's seen me here."

Sally turned to face her. "Can you see, Annie? Can you see now?"

"Not well, but . . ." Annie then whispered, "I don't want them to know that my sight is returning. I can't see clearly right now, just shadows and some colors, light and dark. The way I understand it, it's the fact that I'm blind that fascinates them, so it's best they don't know my sight is returning. I won't be of any use to them anymore."

Sally kissed her cheek. "I won't tell."

Annie smiled, for the first time in many weeks. It dawned on her that she had not smiled since that evening when she sat on Luke's lap telling him about the coming baby. How long ago was that? Who were those people? They did not exist anymore.

She hugged Sally tightly. "Oh, Sally, I can't believe this. This is the only happiness I've known in such a long time!"

"Me too." Sally rested her head on Annie's shoulder. "Do you think the Shawnee will stay here all winter?"

"I have no doubt. It's getting colder, and Indians usually stay put in winter. I remember Jeremiah saying that. And that's a good thing for us. It will be easier for Jeremiah or Luke to find us if the Shawnee stop moving us around. And for now, we're safe. You're too young to marry, and if they keep thinking I'm blind, I'm safe, too. For now, we just have to cooperate, Sally. Don't do anything to make them angry."

"I won't. I hope they let me stay with you all the time."

"They will if I ask them. There is one woman here who speaks pretty good English. I'll tell her it's my wish to have my sister with me. I'm learning to believe in God again, Sally, because I think He's the one who caused my blindness, so that when the awful attack came, I would be spared. We can't let this destroy our faith in God, Sally."

"But He let Mama be killed. And Pa, too . . . and Cal."

"He didn't do that, Sally. Satan came into the hearts of those men, and it was Satan who caused all that to happen. Finding you alive tells me God is now playing His hand in this. He'll save us, Sally, and He'll protect Luke and Jeremiah and help them find us. Even if Mr. Boone doesn't find them, Jeremiah especially will know where to look for us. He knows all about Indians and where they live in winter."

She wasn't really so sure of that, but she knew she had to give her sister hope. And saying the words filled her own heart with hope. She stroked Sally's hair and hugged her again. "Thank God," she whispered. "Thank you, Mama." She believed her mother's spirit had a hand in leading Sally to her. Now, somehow, Luke or Jeremiah had to learn about what happened at Fort Harmar. If they found out, they would come. Surely, one of them would come.

27

December 20, 1780
Mad River, Present-day Western Ohio

Jeremiah continued on foot, trudging through deep snow that had fallen overnight. His wearied horse had literally dropped dead several days ago, and to Jeremiah, it seemed a sign that everything he'd ever loved was being taken from him. Would the same happen with Annie?

He'd come to the point of walking miles a day, through mountain passes, deep valleys, over frozen lakes . . . then literally falling into the snow at night to pray for guidance and strength. He was not going to give up. His only chance rested in the Shawnee staying in one place for the winter, and that place was Piqua Town, just as Daniel Boone surmised rightly that they would. Thank God the man had seen Annie. Knowing she was there saved him weeks of useless searching.

He guessed that by now, he wasn't far from his destination. He'd been to Piqua Town only once before, on a trip for an English trading company, long before the revolution. He'd struggled to remember the way, as back then he'd traveled with trappers who knew the land better than he did.

He stopped to rip away some soft pine branches from a large tree. They were bent low, burdened with heavy snow. He began twisting and wrapping them together to fashion some snowshoes. Trudging through deep snow was taking too much of a toll on his strength and energy, both of which he would need when he found Annie . . . and he *would* find her, or die trying!

As he worked, he wondered how men got themselves into so much trouble. Was it just man's nature to always be fighting someone? What was it that led men to go into dangerous country to make homes for themselves? What made a man wander and explore and go beyond safe boundaries?

If he knew the answer, he would know how to stop these trying events, how to stop himself from always leaving people . . . hurting people. He'd sure enough hurt Annie all those years ago . . . and he'd hurt both Annie and Luke by leaving during these dangerous times.

A strong wind rushed through the pines, shaking the branches and causing more snow to fall on him. He shook it away and kept working, his anger over the war and his own mistakes helping him ignore the cold that chilled him to the bone.

He finished the snowshoes, and by then, the sun was beginning to set. That was another problem at this time of year. There were fewer daylight hours during which to search. He tied the snowshoes to his winter moccasins, moccasins Shara had made for him when he stopped at her village on his way to search for Annie. He was glad to discover she'd indeed married a Delaware warrior. Jimmy Bear had helped outfit Jeremiah fully for winter, and now Jeremiah owed the Delaware his life twice over.

He managed to get in another mile or so before he knew he'd better find shelter for the night. Ahead of him lay the Mad River, and surprisingly, it was not yet frozen. It was, however, flowing very slowly, with chunks of ice in the water. He saw a fallen tree nearby and figured he could get across by floating on its trunk. It wouldn't be easy, but Piqua Town was on the other side. He had no choice but to cross the river.

The opposite bank posed another serious problem. The land rose straight up from the river's edge. He'd have to walk quite a distance in one direction or another to find a better place to climb up.

He'd worry about that in the morning. For now, he could see a cavelike indentation at the bottom of the opposite bank, a place where a man could huddle out of the wind and snow. There was probably plenty of brush over there to make a fire, and with the bank being so high, it was doubtful that the Shawnee would even notice the smoke, since Piqua Town was a couple of miles farther off.

He pushed and rolled and tugged at the fallen tree trunk until he managed to get it most of the way into the river. By then, his lungs burned from his heavy breathing of cold air, and he felt ice at the end of his nose. Dreading the frigid water, he straddled the tree trunk and pushed and yanked and wiggled it farther into the water until the current took over. He pulled his musket loose and used it like a paddle, sometimes managing to shove it into the river bottom to push himself along, glad that the river was not too wide or deep. By the time he reached the other side, he had to paddle more fiercely, since suddenly the bottom took a drop and he couldn't reach it with his musket. The trunk floated past the hole in the side of the bank.

"Come on! Come on!" he growled, his feet becoming numb from the cold. He paddled desperately until finally the front end of the trunk caught in some brush and took hold. Jeremiah managed to shimmy along the trunk and grab hold of the brush, then jump waist-deep into the water, crying out from the awful cold as he waded to shore. On feet he could barely feel, he walked back to the cavelike hole and removed a rolled-up bearskin from his shoulders, thanking God it was still mostly dry. He wrapped himself in it and huddled into the hole, which he guessed was big enough for at least two people.

It was surprisingly warm in there, out of the wind, and that gave him an idea. Perhaps God was on his side in his determination to find and help Annie. If He was, the Shawnee didn't know about this hole in the side of the riverbank.

28

December 21, 1780
North Carolina

Luke found himself involved in the southern campaign after refusing to take part in a mutinous act in Pennsylvania. At least
fifteen hundred American soldiers there had seized Princeton in
a grievance over back pay. The new American government was
broke.

Luke didn't really care. He hadn't joined the cause for
money. He'd joined to kill Loyalists, and those with whom he
now traveled had come here on word that a guerrilla campaign
was being planned in the South, where the British still held their
strongest positions. He and those with him had great respect for
General Nathanael Greene, whom George Washington himself
had appointed commander in the South. Greene in turn had
assigned special guerrilla movements to a man named Henry Lee,
whom some called Light-Horse Harry.

This was what Luke had been waiting for—surprise attacks
on Loyalists and Tories! He could only hope that some of those
he would help to kill would be the same men who'd conducted
the ugly raids on his farm and at Willow Creek.

For the past two weeks, he and Preacher Falls, along with the only two remaining men from Willow Creek who'd first left for this venture, had been taking part in special training maneuvers—practicing better marksmanship, learning to paint their faces to hide them from the enemy, and working on running while reloading their muskets at the same time. Luke remembered how good Jeremiah had always been at that. By the time he finished this training, he'd be just as good as his brother. It all reminded him that he and Jeremiah were more alike after all than Luke always felt.

They had their father's blood in them, the blood of a man who'd fight to the death for what was right, or in defense of his family. Right now, Luke felt he was doing both. If the Loyalists won this war, God only knew the extent of the havoc they would wreak against the Patriots and their families, maybe for years to come. They could use treason as an excuse to claim everything anyone affiliated with the Patriots owned. The only way for himself and others like him—all those who had risked their lives and fortunes to settle this land—to have true freedom to run this country the way it should be run was to defeat the British for once and for all and have their own government.

He stood at attention now, listening to Henry Lee make an announcement.

"Gentlemen!" he shouted to the five hundred or so men gathered in a chilly wind. He stood on a small rise so that most of the men could see and hear him. "George Washington and our new government want to thank you for your loyalty. Some of you know that Patriot soldiers up in Pennsylvania committed mutiny, demanding back pay. Their grievances have been heard, but proving their enlistment dates has been difficult. Now, I ask you, which ones of you joined the Continental Army for the money?"

No one raised a hand. Lee smiled in apparent satisfaction. "Just as I thought!" The man strutted in his gold-colored pants and vest, topped by a dark-blue uniform coat with tails and gold lapels, gold-fringed epaulettes decking his shoulders and making them appear wider than they really were.

"For that, I admire you!" the man went on. "You are exactly the kind of men we need. And just so you know, the American government has managed a loan from the Netherlands. Between that and help from the French, both monetary and in troops and warships, we *will* win this war!" He studied them for a moment, then smiled again. "You may relax and cheer if you like."

With that, Luke and the others broke into a din of cheering and shouting, some men raising their muskets, some whistling, others beginning a chant that caught on.

"Liberty or death! Liberty or death! Liberty or death!"

Luke joined them, recognizing the words as taken from a speech by the now-famed Patrick Henry, who was among those men who first called for independence. His speech had been published, and one publication led to another until just about everyone in the country had read it somewhere. Luke had never believed those words more than now.

"Liberty or death!" he shouted with the others. Finally, Light-Horse Harry held up his hand for silence and the men stopped their chanting. After giving them a moment to quiet down, Lee continued his talk.

"Most of you know our purpose, but some of you are probably still confused. We have been training you hard, and that is because to finish this war, we need the best, most dedicated, well-trained men we can find. And just so you know what lies ahead, you will be split into two smaller groups, one under Brigadier General Daniel Morgan, and one under Lieutenant Colonel William Washington, a cousin to the commander-in-chief himself!"

Several of the men clapped and shouted, "George Washington forever!"

Once they quieted down again, Lee continued. "You will be fighting a guerrilla war," he told them. "It will be dangerous, but very satisfactory, and we intend it to be very effective. You will instigate surprise attacks, just like the Tories have committed surprise attacks against your own families. They will live to regret those attacks!"

Once again the crowd of men cheered, Luke included.

"This will not be easy," Lee continued. "Sometimes we will be fighting and hiding in swampy land. There is a lot of that here in the South, but you have been trained in how to handle such obstacles. Luckily, the weather is not so cold as in the North. We'll have many cool, damp days like this one, but seldom the freezing-cold blizzards like they're currently having up there. And I promise you that with the loan from the Netherlands, it will not be long before we will be able to outfit all of you with better muskets and new uniforms!"

The men started to cheer again, but Lee held up his hand. "However," he continued, "in guerrilla warfare, some of you will not be able to wear uniforms. You will live in swamps and behind trees and in foxholes. You will wear plain clothing so as not to attract too much attention and not to show color amid the trees. We have spies and scouts who will keep us informed of where Loyalists are meeting and hiding, and we will clean them out like rats from behind walls!"

Now he let them cheer again. Deep inside, Luke wondered if he could ever again be the "old" Luke—the farmer, the husband, and the peacemaker. He supposed a lot of that would depend on Annie, how she felt about things when he returned . . . and if she could forgive him for leaving.

29

December 21, 1780
Piqua Town

Jeremiah took a telescope from where it was tied at his waist and pulled it open. A bright morning sun hit the snow just right for a good view of Piqua Town, a grand mixture of longhouses, conical huts, log homes and trading posts, and even a few buildings made of brick and stone. Annie could be anywhere.

He held up the long instrument and scanned the establishment for several minutes. Smoke climbed lazily from smoke holes in the longhouses, from chimneys in the log homes, and there were even some cooking fires outside. Horses were penned in large, fenced areas to the south. Dogs ran about, as did some children.

Jeremiah wondered if perhaps he should just walk right into the camp posing as a trapper/trader. Still, for that, he should have a horse and supplies. They might not believe a man on foot carrying little but his own weapons and a bedroll. And the Shawnee were unpredictable. They might welcome him as a friend and trader, or they might decide they were getting bored with being holed up for the winter and choose to use him for entertainment in gleeful torture. There was no doubt he'd suffer the latter once they knew he intended to steal away one of their captives.

He decided the best thing to do was to wait till dark and move in closer. One thing he knew how to do was sneak around as well as the sneakiest of Indians, and if he left his hair long and straight, simple glimpses of him moving about might not even raise suspicion. He hardly looked different from most of the Shawnee men walking about, except that his leggings were ankle-length, not knee-length. With that thought, he took out his hunting knife, cut off several of the rawhide fringes along the sides of his leggings and tied them together to make two longer cords. Then he rolled up his leggings to the tops of his knee-high fur moccasins and used the leather cords to tie them off there. He then removed his jacket and the two deerskin shirts he wore for insulation. Under these he wore a common calico shirt, which he proceeded to rip into strips. He tied the strips around his head turban-style to make himself look even more like a Shawnee man. Shivering, he then put his deerskin shirts and fur jacket back on.

He spent the rest of the day hovering in the trees, glad that the clouds made their appearance and toned down the shadows and colors. The day had been so bright and sunny that he'd feared being spotted amid the trees. He gradually made his way around the entire settlement, using his telescope to spy on each angle. In late afternoon, he watched a few young girls playing some kind of tag game. One of them lost her fur hat, and Jeremiah nearly gasped aloud. Her hair was red! Astounded, he watched only the red-haired girl with his telescope. She looked so familiar.

"Sally!" he finally whispered. Few young girls had hair that red.

The thought brought quick pain to his heart, as Annie, too, had pretty red hair. Now there was nothing left of her family but Sally . . . and, he hoped to God, Annie herself. He lowered the telescope, his heart pounding with gladness. Thank God Sally was still alive! If Annie was, too, he now had a new problem . . . getting *two* captives away from here instead of just one.

He crept closer, using the telescope again to watch Sally until finally she ran inside a conical dwelling. He decided it was likely that if Annie was still here, she would be in that same lodge. He closed the telescope and retied it to his waist, then picked up his musket and moved farther away, using the next long hours to plan his move . . . and to pray. The sun came out again, shedding just enough warmth to melt most of the snow of the day before. The ground itself was not yet solidly frozen.

That was a good sign. God was helping him. Once he ran off with Annie and Sally, the snow would have made it too easy to track them. He prayed that both women were physically strong enough for what they would have to do.

He waited . . . and waited. He heard laughter, smelled meat cooking. He crept closer again, noticed a young girl come out of the same dwelling in which Sally had gone. Taking out his telescope, he watched again. It was Sally, and she was coming this way! Not wanting to startle her and make her scream, he crept behind the thick pines. She kept coming closer, and to his delight, she walked right past him!

Jeremiah reached out, planting a hand around her mouth and pinning her arms with his other hand. He pulled her, kicking and trying to scream, behind the pines. "Sally!" he whispered gruffly. "It's me! Jeremiah! Don't scream!" He waited for her to stop kicking, allowing her to look and see who it was. Her blue eyes widened in shock, and he slowly removed his hand. Smiling, Sally softly squealed his name and hugged him around the neck.

"Jeremiah! Jeremiah! Annie said you or Luke would come, or maybe both of you. Is Luke with you?"

"No. Luke is off fighting with the Patriots somewhere."

"Oh, Jeremiah, how did you find us?" Sally asked, still hugging him.

"That's a long story. How is Annie? Is she all right?"

Grinning from ear to ear, Sally sat back and studied him with dancing eyes. "Yes! They think she's special because she's blind. Did you know that?"

"Yes. I heard."

"But she's getting better, Jeremiah! She can see now, not real good. Things are blurry, she says, but she can make out people and trees and such. She just can't see people's faces clearly."

Jeremiah closed his eyes. "Thank God," he said with a deep sigh. "Is she staying in the same lodge I saw you come from?"

"You saw me before now?"

"Yes. I've been watching you half the afternoon, watching where you went inside. Is that where Annie is?"

"Yes. They actually let us stay there by ourselves. Annie says she thinks they aren't watching us very much because it's winter, and they think we wouldn't try to escape in winter, and because they treat us very well, why would we want to leave? They are good to Annie because they think she has special spiritual powers and is able to read dreams and such."

Jeremiah grinned, pinching her chin lightly. "Well then, God Himself is watching over both of you. He led me here, and He's made sure you aren't being watched. I have a plan, Sally. You have to tell Annie about it, and you both have to be dressed and ready to run tonight. Understand?"

"Yes! But I have to get back quickly or they will wonder where I went. I came out here to . . . I have to . . . you know."

"Fine." Jeremiah let go of her and stood up, turning around. "Go ahead. I won't look."

He waited while Sally urinated. She walked around in front of him when she finished, her face red. "Thank you for coming, Jeremiah. I can't wait to tell Annie you're here to rescue us!"

"Well, that hasn't happened yet. We have to pray we can manage this. As soon as you think it's safe, I want you and Annie to come out here tonight, to this very spot. To help you out, I'm going to set fire to some of the longhouses to create confusion. Can you remember exactly where to come?"

"Yes!"

"Just wait till the fires start, and be ready to run. And for now, don't look too happy when you go back, all right? Don't give yourself away."

Sally nodded. "I won't." She hugged Jeremiah again. "Thank you! Thank you!" she told him, her eyes tearing. She hurried off then, and Jeremiah watched after her.

"God help us," he muttered, sitting down to again wait for darkness to come.

30

A cold wind picked up, rushing through the pines with a loud moan. Jeremiah scraped flint against stone and lit two dead pine branches he'd picked up. Crouching behind a longhouse, he touched one of the branches to it and set it afire. Quickly, he moved to another, then to a conical house, then another longhouse. In moments, the long-dried wooden lodges flared into rapid burning. Women began screaming as they fled the flames with their children.

Perfect! The confusion would be a big help. Naturally, the Shawnee would expect Sally and Annie to run out of their own house for fear that it, too, might catch fire. He stayed to the shadows as he ran back to the place he'd told Sally to meet him with Annie, then waited and watched, praying that the two would find the opportunity to get away unseen.

He worried over the fact that the clouds had again vanished and the bright, full moon shining against the snow through leafless trees would make them easy to follow, especially for experienced trackers like the Shawnee. The only saving grace was the fact that no more snow had fallen and now that the colder night air had settled, the ground and the fallen leaves had turned to a hard crust. That meant their feet would not sink into anything deeply. They would not leave a readily readable trail, but it didn't take much for Indians to smell out their prey. He could do it himself, but his own knowledge helped him know what to do to leave the least amount of evidence to follow. And, all important, it was dark.

"Come on," he whispered, watching the dwelling where he knew Annie and Sally were. The fires grew larger. Men, women, and children ran everywhere. Horses whinnied. Dogs barked. Some of the Shawnee began beating at the flames with blankets. Others ran with baskets and buckets to a nearby stream.

Finally, he saw them, two dark figures emerging from around the side of the conical house where Annie and Sally lived. One of the figures was taller than the other.

"Annie!" he whispered, his heart pounding. What shape was she in? What had the horrible attack done to her? He guessed her to be a damn strong woman, someone who could rise above the worst of events and overcome anything man and nature might throw at her. He could only pray that Luke was still alive and that somehow his brother and Annie and Sally could find happiness again. One thing was sure: if Luke was still alive, then he himself would have to leave Annie forever after this. He was rescuing her as much for Luke as for Annie. If he died doing it, so be it. He deserved it.

They came closer . . . closer.

"Jeremiah," Sally called out. With all the confusion and screaming going on behind them, it was easy to speak out and not be heard.

Jeremiah let out a soft whistle, and the two sisters headed his way. Moments later, Jeremiah was wrapping his arms around Annie, who literally collapsed against him in tears.

"Oh, my God," she whimpered. "Jeremiah! Jeremiah! You found us!"

"Hush," he whispered, pressing her close. "There's no time to talk about any of this, Annie. We've got to run!" He rocked her for a moment, then leaned down to kiss her cheek. "I know you can hardly see. You've just got to trust me, Annie. I won't let go of you."

"Jeremiah..."

He wiped at the tears on her cheeks. "No crying. There's no time for it now. Are you ready?"

She sniffled and nodded her head. "Yes," she whispered.

"Let's go!" Jeremiah grabbed Sally about the waist and took hold of Annie's hand and started running. The bright moon he feared would give them away now made it easier to avoid tree limbs and debris that might trip them up. Behind them, the screaming and barking and whinnying continued, the noise dimming as they ran...and ran. Annie fell. Jeremiah stopped to help her to her feet.

"I can't keep up with you!" she lamented.

"I'll slow down. And damn it, I'll carry you, too, if I have to."

"Jeremiah, they'll kill you! They'll torture you to death!"

"Not if they don't find us!"

"But how—"

"Don't worry. How many times do I have to tell you to trust me, woman?"

Off they went again, but moments later, they heard war cries behind them.

"Jeremiah! Someone must have seen us!"

"Get down! Get down!" Jeremiah led them behind a pine tree. "Stay here!"

"Oh, God!" Annie whimpered. "They'll kill you! They'll kill you!"

"Hush!" Jeremiah waited and listened, while Sally softly

whimpered in terror and Annie's breathing was labored. The voices came closer, and through the pine branches, Jeremiah could see three warriors. Only three. He didn't want to use his musket. Its fire would draw attention. Maybe the rest of the village didn't even know yet that Sally and Annie were gone. If he could take care of these three . . .

He pulled his tomahawk from its cord at his waist, and quickly rising, he flung it. It landed with a thud in the chest of one of the warriors. Instantly, Jeremiah leaped from his cover, hunting knife in hand. He suspected the warriors were looking only for Sally and Annie, not realizing a "white warrior" was with them. He used their startled confusion to his advantage, running up and ramming his knife into the back of one of the others, who'd turned to see if someone was behind him. He felt something slice across his own back and whirled, lashing out with his hunting knife to catch the third warrior across the face. The man cried out and came at Jeremiah. Both men tumbled to the ground, the warrior on top of Jeremiah and each man trying to ward off the other's knife. The Shawnee warrior managed to turn his knife slightly to begin cutting through Jeremiah's coat and into his arm, but Jeremiah ignored the stinging pain.

With a surge of rage, Jeremiah managed to rear up and force the Shawnee man onto his back. He planted his knee on the man's chest, pushing hard to keep him from breathing. In moments, the man weakened, and Jeremiah jerked his knife hand away, slicing his own knife across the warrior's throat, silencing him forever.

He got up then and shoved his knife into its sheath. Hurrying over to yank his tomahawk out of the first Indian's chest, he shoved that, too, back into his belt and called out for Annie and Sally. "Come on!"

"Jeremiah, I saw one of them cut you!" Annie said, running up to him.

"Doesn't matter right now. I just have to hope I'm not bleeding so much that it will come through my clothing and drip on the ground. If I don't leave a blood trail, we might still get away!"

Wincing from the pain in his back, he picked Sally up like a log again, holding her fast under his right arm as he took Annie's hand and resumed running. He was glad for winter clothing. Otherwise, the slice to his back would have gone much deeper, perhaps cutting his spinal cord and killing him.

After several minutes, he sensed Annie slowing again.

"Jeremiah, I'm so sorry!" she told him.

"It's all right. It's not like you've spent your whole life running through the woods like a wild animal." He grabbed her about the waist and half-carried her then, begging God to help him keep going. They only had to make the river. The river.

Jeremiah had no idea where his strength came from as he began to literally carry both woman and girl. After several more minutes, they finally reached the edge of the high cliff on the west riverbank, the one that had been too high for him to climb the day before. He stopped there to catch his breath.

"Jeremiah, you're killing yourself!" Annie worried.

"Better than dying at the hands of the Shawnee," he answered. "Come on! I think we have enough time that you two can walk on your own."

"Where are we going?"

"You'll see." Jeremiah led them along the top of the cliff for a good half mile, then downward as the ground itself sloped to a lower elevation. Here the ground between the rise and the river sloped more gently. "Take it easy," he told the other two. "We've got to get down to the river."

Annie and Sally obeyed, the three of them clinging to trees and shrubbery as they half-slid, half-fell to the riverbank below. Once there, Jeremiah led them into the freezing water.

"I know this is hard," he told them, "but it's the only way to try to fool them. They can't track us through the river. I know a place where we can hide out for a couple of days. When they get to the river, they'll think we went across. They might do the same and keep trying to find us. When they realize there's no trail to follow on the other side, they'll give up. We just have to hope the three of us don't freeze to death before that."

He took their hands and led them along the river's edge. Sometimes they fell into deeper holes, the water coming up to their waists, and even higher for poor Sally. The water was so cold that it did not take long for Jeremiah to be unable to feel his feet and legs. He knew it would be the same for Sally and Annie. He prayed they would not have frostbite to deal with as well as his own wounds.

For that near half mile, they stayed in the water, until by the bright moonlight, Jeremiah recognized their destination—the cavelike hole along the bank where he'd spent the previous night. "Come on." He led Annie and Sally out of the water and to the little cutout. "Climb in. I left my bedroll in there. Take off your wet moccasins and wet skirts and get into the dry blankets."

The two women did as they were told, stripping off the winter moccasins and wet animal-skin skirts the Shawnee had given them. Outside, Jeremiah gathered brush to whisk away any prints left along the narrow beach they'd walked across to reach the shelter. Then he used the brush to cover the entrance. In the darkness, he removed his own wet moccasins and leggings, wiggling out of them but leaving on his long underwear. He moved under the blankets with Sally and Annie.

"We've got to keep our bodies together for warmth," he told

them. "We might have to stay here a day or two, till they give up searching. They'll think we crossed the river—at least I hope that's what they'll think. They'll never figure us to double back like this and stay so close. That's what I'm counting on."

The three of them huddled together under the blankets, Annie's back pressed against Jeremiah, Sally's back against Annie. Jeremiah moved one leg over both of them. "Let's keep rubbing each other's feet for a while. At least we're out of the wind here." He moved his arms around Annie and Sally both.

Annie turned her head slightly. "How can we ever thank you, Jeremiah?" she whispered. "You've risked your life for us."

"It's the least I could do...considering," he answered. "Thank God you're alive," he whispered.

"Jeremiah," she said, sounding as though she was about to cry.

"Try to rest. God knows, we'll need our strength for the journey ahead, if we're lucky enough to get out of here alive."

They settled in for the long wait.

31

December 22, 1780

A shaft of light shone into the cave dwelling where Annie, Sally, and Jeremiah slept. Annie awoke first, and it took her a moment to remember where they were and that Jeremiah himself lay pressed against her back.

Jeremiah! He'd risked everything to save her and Sally. He'd fought three Shawnee braves single-handedly and had suffered a wound because of it, yet he'd half-carried her and Sally all the way here.

The wound! Maybe he wasn't sleeping at all! Maybe he'd bled to death overnight! Afraid of the worst, she turned over to face him, and to her relief, she felt his warm breath on her face. She touched his cheek.

"Jeremiah," she whispered. "Are you awake? Are you all right?"

He took hold of her hand and brought it to his lips, kissing it. "I'm awake. My back hurts, but I think it's just a flesh wound," he said softly, "combined with the normal aches I always feel."

She could see better this morning, just enough to know his

eyes were open . . . those dark eyes that were always so unread-
able. How she wished she could see them better now. She didn't
have to see well to know how handsome he looked, even after
the struggles of the night before. A wildness emanated from
his very being. In spite of all she'd suffered, here was her Jeremiah . . . always the same . . . always brave and wild and rugged
and . . .

"I don't know what to say . . . how to thank you," she told
him.

He leaned close and kissed her cheek. "Just finding you alive
is all that matters. When I heard what happened—the attack,
your blindness, losing the baby—God, I'm sorry, Annie. My
coming home might have caused some of it. If I hadn't left again,
maybe I could have helped somehow."

"It's done now," she whispered, "and there's no going back
and changing any of it. I just . . . it feels so good to lie here with
someone strong who loves me and will take me home."

He touched her hair. "I still love you, Annie. I always will,"
he told her softly. "When I heard what happened . . . God, Annie,
let me take away some of the horror."

"Jeremiah . . ."

He moved on top of her, reaching over then to lay an extra
blanket over Sally. "She's sleeping hard," he told Annie.

Annie knew what he meant. Why couldn't she resist? She
realized that in taking off her Shawnee skirt, she was naked from
the waist down. Shawnee women did not wear drawers as white
women did.

"Jeremiah, right now I don't know who I am . . . where I
belong."

"You are Annie Wilde, and those men didn't touch you. Do
you understand? They didn't touch you."

Annie shivered. What was she doing? She felt so desperate,

so alone, so afraid, so bewildered. And Luke had left her . . .
"Take it all away, Jeremiah," she whispered.

Why did she feel this had to be done, in spite of her love
for Luke? Somehow, this moment seemed right. She felt so abandoned by Luke. He'd left her in her darkest hour.

She let Jeremiah settle between her legs, and when he
reached down to take his swollen penis from the opening of his
long johns, the back of his hand touched her most private place.
In the next moment, Annie drew in her breath as Jeremiah entered her in a hard, hot thrust that made it difficult not to cry
out his name. She forced herself to be still because of Sally.

Quietly, they mated, his glorious manhood ramming deep,
reclaiming what once he'd claimed so many years ago. At the
same time, he erased the ugliness of the rape attack.

He met her mouth in a groaning kiss, and Annie could see
the shadow of his long black hair falling around her. His power
overcame any inhibitions she might have had, and brought back
the memory of how much she'd once loved this man.

Quietly, she arched up to him, glorying in his thrusts, knowing it was wrong, just like the first time, yet wanting to give
something back to this man who'd risked so much to find her.
His kisses were hot and demanding, and she was powerless
against him. It didn't matter.

She felt his life surge into her, and when he was finished,
he just lay there for a few quiet minutes, holding his weight off
of her by resting on his elbows.

"I love you, Annie," he repeated softly.

Tears filled her eyes. "I would have followed you anywhere,
Jeremiah."

He kissed her eyelids. "I didn't think it was fair to take you
to the places I meant to go, or to marry you when I had such a

passion to run off and join the revolution. If I hadn't been taken prisoner aboard that ship, who's to say I still wouldn't have stayed away for some other reason? I was a stupid, confused young man who didn't know what the hell he wanted." Finally, he rolled away from her. "Luke always knew what he wanted, from the very beginning. He wanted to build the farm, and he wanted you. He was by far the better man, and he still is."

Annie closed her eyes. Luke! Where was he? "If we make it to safety, promise me you'll look for him, Jeremiah. Make him come home. Tell him I'm getting my sight back. He was such a changed man when he left, so full of anger and revenge. He wasn't my Luke at all." She wiped at more tears. "And God knows, I'm not myself either. My God, what have we done?"

He pulled her close. "We've comforted each other in a terrible time." He kissed her cheek and rolled farther away from her, rubbing at his eyes. "Once we leave here, we'll find the closest settlement and get help and supplies, then head for Philadelphia. I have friends there who will gladly put up you and Sally safely while I'm gone. We'll leave word with the few people left at Fort Harmar and Willow Creek where you'll be, in case Luke goes back there to look for you. One way or another, I'll find him, or he'll find you . . . if he's alive."

Annie wanted to cry, her emotions ran so strong. How painful it was to be in love with two men, and to be loved by both of them. "Then what?" she asked. "What will you do, Jeremiah?"

He sighed deeply and lay quietly for a moment. "I don't know. Go west, I suppose, really far west . . . maybe scout for the government. I'd like to see what's out there, Annie, see all of the Great Lakes, see what kind of land lies west of there even. If I find Luke and the two of you . . . ." He paused. "I'll have to get

away and not come back, Annie. You understand that, don't
you?"

She blinked back tears. "Of course I do."

"I'll never forget you. Never."

"Nor I you," she whispered. She stared at the low, rocky
ceiling of the small cave. "What if Luke is dead?"

Jeremiah sighed, grasping her hand under the blanket.
"Then I will stop my wandering. I'll stay with you, marry you,
as much for Luke as for you and me. He'd want that. He'd
never want you to be alone and afraid."

"Thank you," she whispered, shivering with tears.

Jeremiah squeezed her hand, and she reveled in the safety
of his presence. Sally woke up then, bolting upright, as though
frightened.

"Annie!"

Jeremiah sat up and reached out to put a hand over her
mouth, pushing her down. "Hush, Sally. We're still safe. Just
don't talk above a whisper."

Sally turned and hugged Annie, who rolled over and pulled
her sister into her arms. "We'll be all right, Sally," she said, wiping away her own tears. "We have to stay here until we're sure
it's safe to go on. Then Jeremiah will take us to Philadelphia,
where we can stay with a family he knows there."

Sally sniffled against her shoulder. Suddenly, Jeremiah put
his arms around both of them and hugged them tightly. "Quiet!"
he whispered. "Don't say another word!"

Annie squeezed Sally tighter as she heard voices. She recognized the Shawnee tongue, even recognized the voice of Cornstalk! Fear gripped her, more for Jeremiah than for herself. If
they were found, the horror it would mean for Jeremiah was too
much to consider.

They waited. The Shawnee men talked loudly, and it sounded to Annie as though they were cursing. She couldn't understand the words, but she could certainly understand the tone of their voices. One walked right by the brush-covered entrance to their little cave. She was so gripped with terror that she could barely breathe or swallow. She could feel Sally shaking almost violently, but Jeremiah's grip remained strong and solid.

The minutes dragged on. More voices, more lamenting and cursing. She jumped when one warrior nearby kicked the dirt and actually sent sand flying through the brush and onto them. Jeremiah hugged them even tighter.

Finally, the voices started to fade. Minutes later, they heard nothing.

"Stay put," Jeremiah whispered. "They could still be out there waiting to see if we make an appearance from somewhere."

"What did they say?" Annie asked.

"They're angry as hell, said we must have already crossed the river. That's what I was hoping for. We just might have a chance, but we don't dare leave here for at least another night. I have some jerked meat and a canteen of water. We'll get by."

"What if we have to . . . you know . . . pee," Sally squeaked, still sniffling.

"Then we'll do it right here. We have no choice. Once we dress and leave, we have to cross the river anyway. The water will wash the filth away. This is no time for modesty. It's a time just to stay alive."

Sally jerked in another sob. "I already wet myself," she whimpered. "I was so scared for you, Jeremiah."

"It's all right, Sally." Annie kissed her hair. "It's going to happen to all of us." She turned her head just enough to look at Jeremiah, and he leaned down and kissed her once more.

Annie already ached at the thought of the day Jeremiah

would once again walk out of her life—probably forever the next time. He'd just become an intense part of her life again, just reawakened her to safety and warmth and love and the beauty of sharing her body with a man, erasing the ugly filth of her attackers. She should feel horrible guilt again, like her guilt over that night in the barn with him. But that was another Annie. Strangely, she didn't feel guilty this time. The fact that she and Jeremiah had so easily and quickly mated only told her how natural and good their love could have been . . . in another time . . . another place.

32

February 1, 1781
South Carolina

Luke moved as stealthily as an Indian, making his way toward the camp where scouts told him and those with him that Loyalists were entrenched, planning their next move against Patriotic families. What was it about men and war that made those who would not think of killing another human being suddenly turn into murderers? That's what some Loyalists and Tories had been doing. Now he'd been doing the same thing in return.

At least their own attacks were only against war camps, not innocent families. He had that much to convince himself this was right. If they didn't deliver a solid message to Loyalists and get rid of as many of them as possible, the English would simply have the support of such men and the war would last that much longer.

It was time to end this hideous mess. He'd lost track of how many men he'd already killed, and with each one, he pictured the men who'd destroyed his farm, his wife's honor, her eyesight. Somehow, he had to find a way to end his own anger and hatred and go home to Annie . . . his Annie.

How was she now? And what had made him think she'd
be truly safe at Fort Harmar? What if she wasn't? With so many
men gone off to war, wouldn't this be a good time for the Indians
to retake land they still considered their own? The frontier had
been weakened, and Indians could smell that out like a bobcat
could smell wounded prey.

Why hadn't he considered that? He'd been so full of rage
and frustration, he'd failed to think straight. Now all he could
think of were Annie's tears, how she'd begged him not to go. If
he got back to find out something worse had happened, or that
she'd been killed, he'd want to die himself. What would he have
left to live for anyway, with Annie gone . . . his farm gone . . . his
whole life destroyed?

He and the others drew closer. He'd committed himself to
this for now. Henry Lee, and the men with him now, depended
on him keeping that commitment. Still, he'd been committed to
Annie, too, and he'd broken that commitment, letting war become more important. He wasn't even sure anymore of what
drove him to continue with the guerrilla raids, other than the
need to make sure men like their enemies could not go on to
rape and kill more innocent people.

Several Tories and Loyalists sat around a campfire not far
away. His face painted black with ashes, Luke snuck closer, musket and bayonet ready. His assignment was to storm a designated
tent and kill everyone inside before they had a chance to defend
themselves. Others had similar assignments, while the rest would
attack the men sitting around the fire.

He heard the soft whistle, and in the next moment, he and
thirty other men surrounding the camp ran like hell at the Loyalists, raising war whoops like wild Indians. Luke ducked and
rolled, noticing several of the men around the fire already falling
from the sudden gunfire of Patriot muskets. In seconds, more

Patriots were on the men, jabbing and ramming bayonets.

Luke ripped his own bayonet across his assigned tent and fired, then began stabbing at those inside. To his horror, a woman screamed just as he rammed yet again. He glanced at the woman, surprised that there was a female in the tent. She stared in terror at his bayonet.

"Murderer!" she wailed. "Murderer! You filthy bastard! Horrible, Patriot child killer!"

Confused, Luke looked down to see he'd bayoneted a young boy, perhaps eight years old. Stunned, he jerked out the bayonet, and blood squirted from the boy's chest. He stumbled backward, watched the killing going on around him, heard yet another woman scream, watched a Patriot soldier shoot her.

His throat began to close. How could this happen? He and these men had turned into the very kind of men they thought they were ridding the country of. Innocent people were dying at their hands! This was not the way it was supposed to be. Within minutes, the men around him were cheering and laughing and celebrating.

Yes, freedom meant everything, but not to the point of this kind of killing. He looked down at his bayonet. Blood! A child's blood! That boy could have been his own son! How much would he have hated those who'd killed him? How was he going to ever be forgiven for this?

"Murderer!" the woman inside continued shouting. "My son! My son! Oh, God, my son!" She stepped through the ripped tent, pointing a small pistol at him. Before he could react, she fired.

Luke felt the sting, thinking how odd it was that the ball that entered him didn't hurt more than that. At first, he thought perhaps the gun was so small that it hadn't done much damage, but suddenly he felt as though he couldn't breathe. The night became blacker, and he felt his legs go out from under him.

33

Annie walked onto the second-story balcony of the fine brick home where she and Sally now lived. Downstairs in the study, Sally was learning to catch up on all the education she'd missed out on by being raised on the frontier. She was being tutored by a male teacher who regularly taught James and Rebecca Stoddard, the children of Arland Stoddard, the wealthy Philadelphia merchant who owned this home.

Stoddard had contributed a good deal of money to the Patriot cause. He was himself too old to take part in the war and was disgruntled by the import and export taxes England tried to force on the colonists. Because of Jeremiah's involvement in the war, and with George Washington, whom Stoddard considered a good friend, Jeremiah had come to know the man well; and just as he'd promised, the Stoddards were more than glad to take in Jeremiah's sister-in-law and her young sister, especially since Jeremiah's own brother had also joined the Patriot cause... somewhere.

Would she ever see Luke again? In spite of her reawakened

love for Jeremiah, Annie ached to find what she and Luke once shared. Jeremiah was leaving in the morning to try to find Luke. She felt desperately torn between the brothers. Her journey here with Jeremiah had been tortuous—freezing cold, blizzards, a struggle to find shelter and help, a long journey through dangerous territory where Tories and Loyalists and Indians could be lurking, ready to attack at any time.

She and Jeremiah had not made love again since that one sweet, almost unreal morning when they hid in the cave. After that, life had been comprised of a struggle to survive until they reached help and were able to make the long journey here to Philadelphia. They hadn't even talked about what they had done, and since arriving here, Jeremiah had been busy going to meetings and finding out what was happening with the war. He stayed at a boarding house on the other side of town, and Annie suspected he had deliberately stayed away as much as possible, coming here only occasionally for dinner.

What they'd gone through brought her and Jeremiah closer, even though they had not shared their bodies again, or even talked about it. There was something special between them now that could never be changed and would never go away. Her dilemma caused headaches and an inability to eat, and worse, she'd not had a period since not long before Jeremiah found her.

She was carrying Jeremiah Wilde's baby? She refused to tell him. Why burden him with that worry when he was going off to war again, headed for more danger? He needed to stay focused on matters at hand, for it could mean his life.

She watched the activity on the brick street below—wagons clattering by, finely dressed women chatting on street corners, some with packages in their hands and wearing fine furs. Mrs. Stoddard was a small woman, hardly bigger than Annie, and so Annie was able to wear her dresses.

She looked down at the brown-velvet dress she wore now, so warm she hardly needed more than a shawl on this sunny day in spite of the cold. She'd never dressed so finely in her life, hardly even realized clothes like this existed. This was a life she'd never known, not even when she lived here in the East as a child. How different all this was from the dangerous and rugged frontier.

She could hardly remember the woman who'd married Luke Wilde only seven months ago. It seemed more like years ago. Fate had stepped in to change everything, and the farm and the fine home she'd had there seemed like a distant dream. The happiness she'd known with Luke...the joy of that evening when she sat on his lap telling him about the baby...had all that really happened? And how in God's name had she survived that awful attack and the terrifying blindness and the sorrow of losing her baby...let alone captivity in a Shawnee camp! Now here she was living in a fine home in Philadelphia, carrying his brother's child! What strange twists in life were still in store for her?

Mama...Father...Calvin...all dead. And what had ever happened to Jake after he left? It would help her heart so much to find her oldest brother and Luke both alive! Jeremiah had promised to do all he could to find both of them, and she knew he'd keep that promise. Still, what could she say to Luke? How could she explain what had happened?

Jeremiah was leaving tomorrow...tomorrow. He most likely would never come back. If he found Luke and/or Jake, he'd send them instead. It would be better that way, but the thought of it made her throat hurt and her eyes tear. What would happen to her and Luke's marriage, a marriage that had hardly been given a chance to even *be* a marriage?

Someone tapped lightly on her door. Annie went inside, closing the French doors to the balcony and walking over to the bedroom door. She opened it to see Jeremiah standing there, handsome as ever, wearing fine black pants and a white ruffled shirt with gathered sleeves. She wondered if any better specimens of man existed than the Wilde brothers, and she couldn't help wondering what their father must have been like. No wonder Jess Wilde had loved Noah so much.

Jeremiah's hair was pulled straight back into a tail at the back of his neck, and his shirt was unlaced at the top, revealing dark skin. He smiled softly, but a terrible sadness shone in his eyes. "No one knows I'm here but the maid, and she won't tell," he told her.

Annie stepped back, knowing that this was his way of asking to come into the room. She closed the door after he entered and faced him.

"You look wonderful, more beautiful than I've ever seen you."

She felt a flush come to her cheeks. "Thank you. And I haven't seen you this way in a long time; no buckskins, no weapons." She smiled. "We certainly are a far cry from the two people who lay huddled in that little cave, aren't we?"

He nodded, his smile fading. "Yes."

Annie knew what he was thinking. They'd made love in that cave. What a strange time and place to find each other again. She looked away, and the air hung still for a moment.

"Annie," he finally spoke up ... at the very same time she spoke his name. The moment seemed suddenly awkward and painful. She remained turned away, and suddenly he was moving his arms around her. "I'll leave in the morning."

"I know." *I'm carrying your child!* She wanted to shout the words. No. She couldn't tell him. "I'll miss you the rest of my life, Jeremiah." She turned then, unable to stop herself from falling against him in tears. "I love you so!" she sobbed.

He wrapped his arms around her, kissing her hair. "And I love you, Annie. And I'll miss you the rest of *my* life, but you know you belong to Luke, and that's as it should be. If I find him alive—"

"Then find him, Jeremiah," she wept. "Find him and send him to me. Find out if he's the Luke I married, and if he still loves me."

"How could he *not* love you? Of course he still does. And I *will* find him. I'll check every hospital, travel to every camp and ask about him. I'll check every roster, and even the English prisons."

"No!" She looked up at him. "They might arrest you again! You still have to be careful, Jeremiah, until this war is over."

He grasped her shoulders. "And it soon will be. Word is that the Patriots are gaining a strong lead. I've learned that the Union has money now, big loans from Spain and the Netherlands. They have better-trained soldiers, and a hell of a lot more determination than the English. England has declared war on the Dutch and is also fighting France. They're stretching themselves too thin, and that's good for us; and that bloody Ban Tarleton was defeated at the Cowpens down in South Carolina, so I'm told. South is where I'll go, Annie. The Patriots are raiding Loyalist strongholds down there. Most of the war is taking place in the Carolinas and Virginia now. That's the most likely place to find both Jake and Luke."

"Please, please be careful, Jeremiah. I don't want you to get hurt or arrested. And if Luke is dead, you're all I have."

"I'll be all right. I'll be extra careful, not for myself but for you."

She watched him lovingly, able to see very clearly now. Oh, that look in his eyes! She wanted him to make love to her again, and she could tell that was exactly what he wanted, too; but the situation was different now. To make love now would be pure, selfish lust, rather than the gentle needs of that morning in the cave.

"I never lost respect for you, Annie," he told her, "not after that first time . . . and not after what happened in that cave. You are one of the strongest women I've ever known, and Luke is a lucky man."

"And I'm a lucky woman . . . to be loved by two such wonderful men." The ache for him brought her physical pain. She grasped his hands and kissed both of them. "Good-bye, Jeremiah. God be with you."

He squeezed her hands. "Good-bye, Annie. My things are at the boarding house where I'm staying. I'll not come back in the morning."

"I know."

He stood there a moment longer, still holding her hands, and Annie suspected he was on the brink of tears. "Tell your children about their Uncle Jeremiah someday," he finally told her.

She nodded. Oh, how she wanted to tell him she might be telling one of her children about his or her own father.

Jeremiah finally turned and went to the door. He hesitated there a moment, and Annie looked at him, saw the pain in his dark eyes. "Bye, Annie."

He walked out, closing the door behind him, and Annie crumpled to the floor in tears.

34

March 15, 1781
South Carolina

Jeremiah found himself in the thick of it, having searched everywhere until becoming involved in the guerrilla warfare of General Nathanael Greene and Lieutenant Colonel Henry Lee, a
brilliant strategist who moved swiftly against England's "Swamp
Fox," Lord Cornwallis, whom the Patriots finally chased out of
the Carolinas into Virginia.

Jeremiah stayed with Lee's men as they headed south to continue cleaning out Loyalists. They marched and chopped their
way through hackberry thickets to attack and take over a place
called Fort Motte from English guerrillas led by a man called
Francis Marion. Fort Motte was really a large plantation in South
Carolina, and the woman who currently owned the place en-
couraged the Patriots to burn her home if that was what it took
to get the English out of it. She even helped ignite the roof, and
the British soldiers came out so fast that the Patriots were able
to put out the fire before it did much damage. To the surprise
and delight of the officers, the amazingly strong and brave Mrs.
Motte then proceeded to entertain the captured British officers

and the Patriots who'd defeated them at her own dinner table! Her bravery reminded Jeremiah of Annie.

Now he camped outside with the victorious Patriots, some of whom danced around campfires while others played their fifes and drummers trumped up a steady rhythm. Jeremiah searched their faces, and one struck him as familiar. He'd seen him only that one day—the day Annie married Luke—but he was almost sure . . .

He walked over to the man, whose face was black from gunpowder. "Preacher Falls?"

The man looked up, frowning. "You look familiar. Fact is, you look a lot like . . . like Luke Wilde!"

Filled with hope, Jeremiah knelt down near the man. "I'm Jeremiah, Luke's brother."

The man grinned with joy. "Of course! Jeremiah! My God, man, where did you come from?"

"It's a long story." Jeremiah put out his hand to return Falls's eager handshake.

"My God," Falls repeated. "Jeremiah! I thought you probably died a long time ago. I suspected Luke helped you escape after those English soldiers took you away, but nobody knew what happened to you after that."

"I've been searching for my brother. Do you have any idea where he is? And have you ever seen Jake Barnes, Annie's brother?"

"Annie! Have you seen her? How are things on the frontier?"

"That's another long story." Jeremiah moved to sit down on a log beside the man. "A very long story. I'll get to it as soon as you tell me what you know about Luke."

The preacher sobered. "He was hurt bad, Jeremiah. About six weeks ago it was. We raided a Loyalist camp and by accident,

Luke killed a young boy. The boy's ma shot Luke in the chest. It was just a pistol, but it did enough damage to put Luke down. I helped carry him back to our camp and he was taken on to the Cowpens. The English had set in there, but we took the Cowpens back in January, you know."

"I heard. Is Luke still there?"

"Most likely. When they left to take him there, he was in a worse state emotionally than physically. Killing that young boy hit him hard. It's not his nature to kill at all, let alone a child. The things that happened back at his farm, it changed him, Jeremiah. I don't think he realized how much till he killed that child. Then it hit him. It would be good if he could talk to you."

Jeremiah could only imagine Luke's agony. "I hope he's still there and I can finally catch up to him." Thank God he had a lead! "What about Jake Barnes? Do you know anything about his whereabouts?"

Preacher Falls shook his head. "I've never run into him or heard anything about him. Wish I had better news." The man ran a hand through his hair. "Tell me about Willow Creek. Should I go back there? I'm getting tired of this war, and I'm wondering if I've done the right thing."

"You have. God would want you to fight for freedom, Preacher, I'm sure. And I'm so glad to find you. I'll leave in the morning for the Cowpens."

"Tell me all that's happened. Tell me about Annie and the people at Fort Harmar. Should I go back? Where is Annie now?"

Jeremiah suggested they go farther away from all the noise and dancing. The two men sat down in a quieter place, and Jeremiah explained the events of the past few months. Preacher Falls lamented the attack on Fort Harmar. "My God, we thought they were safe there. Luke will be devastated to find out what happened. And poor Mrs. Barnes, dying like that. And poor Annie and Sally. Being taken by the Shawnee must have been terrifying."

"At least they were treated well."

Falls sighed. "You're a braver man than I, Jeremiah, going there to rescue them. God knows what you would have suffered at the hands of the Shawnee if you'd been caught. I've seen what they can do."

"I figured it was worth the risk, for Luke's sake," Jeremiah told the man. *And because I love Annie Wilde.* "I couldn't stand the thought of my brother's wife and her sister being with the Shawnee."

"And Annie can see now?"

Jeremiah nodded. "She's staying with friends of mine in Philadelphia. I promised her I'd find Luke, and her brother, if possible. She's safe now, and living well. She'll be all right. She's a strong young woman, just as brave as any man."

"I've always seen that in her. Luke married well."

Jeremiah felt the old ache in his gut. "Yes. He did."

It was a warm night, and both men talked until finally the celebrating died down and men began crawling into their bedrolls. Jeremiah and Preacher Falls did the same, Jeremiah anxious for dawn. He would ride to the Cowpens as fast as he could. He could hardly wait to find Luke, and he prayed that for Annie's sake, his brother would be recovered and doing well when he got there.

35

April 2, 1781
The Cowpens, South Carolina

Luke walked ... and walked. He was determined to regain his strength before returning to Fort Harmar and Annie. The recovery from his wound had been arduous and painful. According to the doctor who'd taken out the lead ball, it had lodged itself in his right lung, which had collapsed. The healing had been almost unbearable as the lung slowly mended and began to fill. Luke had never experienced such pain and hoped to never have to feel it again.

The pain in his heart over killing a child ran a close second. Would he ever be able to get the picture of his bayonet in that boy's chest out of his mind? For a while, he hadn't even wanted to live, thinking God had him shot for good reason. The only thing that kept him going was to envision Annie's face when he returned to her as he'd promised.

He walked the entire perimeter of the Cowpens five times a day. It was the only way he could think of to get back his strength. He'd gained some of the weight he'd lost, and at least now he could walk all five times without feeling weak and dizzy.

That was a great improvement. By God's grace, he'd not suffered any serious infection, something that killed more men than the effects of the initial wounds they suffered. Why he'd been spared, he wasn't sure. That was something he still had to figure out before going home to Annie.

He started back to his own camp when for some reason, he felt compelled to take a second look at an approaching rider. He was tall and dark, and he rode a swaybacked, roan-colored horse that looked as though it could barely carry the man's weight. The sight was almost humorous, and Luke couldn't help watching a moment longer, until his heart began to pound with joy.

Did he dare believe he recognized the man? He wore buckskins, and his hair was black and long, like an Indian's.

"Jeremiah!" he shouted. He laughed, for the first time in months. "Jeremiah! Over here!" He waved his arms, and the man on the horse tried to kick the sorry piece of horseflesh into a faster trot. The horse managed to speed up a little, and before reaching Luke, Jeremiah slid down off the animal to walk up to his brother.

They embraced.

"My God, Jeremiah, where did you come from?"

"I'd need the rest of the day to explain that," Jeremiah told Luke. "God, it's good to see you, brother! I ran into Preacher Falls farther south and he told me what happened to you." He stepped back. "You look pretty good, Luke . . . a little skinny, but healthy. Thank God you're all right!"

"And you look damn good yourself—a whole lot better than the shape you were in when I left you with those Indians last summer! I've been going nuts wondering if you lived through that. I figured that as long as Jimmy Bear never came to say you'd died, you must be okay." He laughed again, studying his wild-looking brother. "I might have figured you to be too ornery to die."

Jeremiah smiled, an odd sadness in his eyes. "You're probably right."

Luke looked past him at the horse. "Where in hell did you pick up that sorry-looking thing?"

"Traded a blanket for her, and I think the owner got the best end of the deal."

"You're right there!"

Jeremiah chuckled, unloading his things from the saddleless horse. "I think I'll let her go to spend her last days in freedom. I wanted something to help me get here faster, but I'm not sure I couldn't have made it on foot just as fast."

Luke smiled and shook his head. "I don't doubt that." He faced Jeremiah. "Where in God's name have you been?"

Jeremiah's smile faded. "All over." Then he sobered even more. "We need to talk, Luke, about a lot of things."

Luke felt a sudden alarm. "What's wrong? Annie? Is it Annie? Have you seen her?"

Jeremiah sighed. "I've seen her." He sat down in the grass, tossing his gear aside. "Can we stay right here and talk, away from the others?"

"Hell, yes." Luke sat down facing his brother. "What's going on, Jeremiah? How in hell do you know about Annie? Is she all right?"

Jeremiah hesitated, pulling at a piece of dried grass and putting it to his lips to chew on it. "She's all right." He faced Luke, and as he talked, Luke's emotions tumbled inside him, a feeling of devastation engulfing him as Jeremiah explained all that had taken place: the attacks on Fort Harmar and on Willow Creek, how Jeremiah learned from Tories that attacks were planned there and went to investigate. Luke could hardly grasp all that had happened, and guilt riddled him.

"My God, Jeremiah, how can I ever thank you for getting Annie and Sally out of there?" he said after hearing about the rescue from the Shawnee. "Do you have any idea of what they would have done to you if they'd caught you?"

"Oh, believe me, I have a better idea than most. I've lived among them, remember."

Luke shook his head, looking away. "I feel like such a failure."

"Why?"

Luke shrugged, facing his brother again. "I fought so hard to help her the day of the attack, but there were just too many of them. You can't imagine how I felt when I realized what they were . . . doing to her . . . and I couldn't do a damn thing about it." He caught a look of sudden rage in Jeremiah's dark eyes.

"I think I can imagine it." Jeremiah looked down at a withering daisy. He picked at it as he spoke. "You did what you could, Luke, and as far as Fort Harmar, you thought Annie was safe. I'm a man, too, you know. I understand why you felt you had to leave and do something about what happened. I probably would have done the same thing."

"But I never should have left her. I wouldn't be surprised if she never forgave me for it."

"She already has. She told me so herself. She just wants you to go to her, Luke. She needs you."

Luke ached for his wife. "I will go to her, but not just yet. I still feel restless, Jeremiah. I . . . I accidentally killed a young boy in a raid a few weeks back. That's how I got hurt. His mother shot me."

"Preacher Falls told me."

Luke studied his brother's eyes, saw the concern there. "What do you think I should do?"

"I think you should first quit blaming yourself for what happened to Annie—and for killing that boy. War is war, Luke. Things happen." An odd hint of guilt seemed to come into Jeremiah's eyes, and he looked away. "Things happen," he repeated. "God knows, you never would have killed that boy if you'd realized he was in that tent." Jeremiah faced him again. "Just like He knows you never would have left Annie if you'd had any idea a raid was coming. Now it's time to forgive yourself and get back to what you need to do. If you aren't ready to face Annie yet, then at least write her a letter to let her know you're okay and where you're going next."

Luke frowned. "Where *am* I going next? You seem to be ready to tell me."

Jeremiah grinned slightly. "Well, since you've come this far and you feel so bad about that boy, why not make it all worth it? Why don't we stick together now and win this damned war so we can *both* go on with our lives?"

Luke gave the suggestion some thought. "Do you think Annie would understand?"

Jeremiah smiled. "I think Annie is capable of understanding just about anything. She's quite a woman, that wife of yours."

Luke nodded. "I know. Thank God she can see again, and thank God that Sally survived, too." He could almost swear he saw tears in Jeremiah's eyes.

Jeremiah suddenly drew in his breath and stood up. "Have you ever heard anything about Annie's brother Jake?" he asked, seeming to want to change the subject.

"No. I have no idea if he's dead or alive."

Jeremiah shook his head. "That's too bad. I told Annie I'd

try to find him, too, but I have no idea where to look." He turned to Luke and put out his hand. Luke grabbed it and let Jeremiah help him to his feet.

"I've been walking every day, trying to get my strength back. A good wrestling match with my brother might help."

"Oh, no you don't," Jeremiah answered, waving him off. "You aren't fully recovered yet, and I'm bone-tired from breaking my neck to get here in record time." He glanced again at the swaybacked horse, which casually grazed nearby. "It appears I also broke my horse's back."

Luke chuckled. "So it does." He studied his Indian-looking brother. "Damn, it's good to see you, Jeremiah. I feel even stronger now. And I agree. Let's finish this goddamn war and get on with life. Word around here is that George Washington himself is going to form a big movement up in New York and head south to Virginia to rout out Cornwallis. What do you say we join them?"

"I say our father would be very happy to see us join up with Washington. Let's do it for his sake."

Luke nodded. "I'll get a letter off to Annie, tell her how much I love her and that I'm coming home as soon as this war is over. That may be sooner than we think." He sighed deeply. "God, I miss her, Jeremiah. I can't wait to see her again. I just . . . I need to do this first."

"Tell her that. She'll wait for you. She's comfortable and safe now."

"Thanks to you." Luke put out his hand again. "Thank you, brother."

Jeremiah looked at his hand as though he wasn't sure he should shake it. Luke couldn't quite make out the sadness in his brother's eyes. Finally, Jeremiah took his hand, squeezing it firmly. "You're welcome."

Luke didn't let go of his hand. "Is there anything you aren't telling me, Jeremiah? Is there some kind of bad news I don't know about?"

Jeremiah stared at him for a long, silent moment. "No. Just stay healthy so you can go home to your wife. Like I said, she needs you, Luke. She loves you more than you know, and what she's been through just made her stronger."

Luke nodded, finally letting go of Jeremiah's hand. "We have a lot to decide once I get back."

Jeremiah leaned down to pick up his things. "Let's find the commander here and see if it's all right to head north. Neither of us is committed to any particular regiment." He put an arm around Luke's shoulders. "Let's go finish this war."

36

Annie helped polish silverware, feeling she owed something to the Stoddards for allowing her to stay so long. Mrs. Stoddard insisted it was not necessary, but Annie would not listen. Besides, she had to keep busy. She had to stop thinking about Luke and Jeremiah, wondering if they were all right, if they were alive or dead.

Every day she walked to the town square to check the rosters of those known dead. God only knew how outdated they were, as it took so long for the latest news to reach them.

Today was an exception to her ritual. Sally had gone out, and Annie had other things to think about—namely, how she was going to explain her pregnancy to Sally and Mrs. Stoddard. She feared that the woman would kick them both out once she discovered her situation. So far, she'd been able to wear her dresses a little looser and hide her growing belly, but it wouldn't be much longer before that would be impossible.

She set down a silver spoon and touched her stomach. Jeremiah's baby was growing inside of her! She wanted to be happy about it, and secretly she was . . . but the consequences once Luke returned might be dire indeed. Would she long for his return only to lose him after all? Would he hate her? Beat her? Somehow, she could not imagine he would do either. Not her Luke. But then, he might return a changed man, the angry, vengeful man he'd been when he left. Worse than hating her, she didn't want him to hate Jeremiah.

How could she explain the feelings she'd had that morning in the cave, her fear and desperation, her terrible need to be held and loved, her wonder if she would ever see Luke again? It made her ill to think of the look she'd see in Luke's handsome blue eyes. For now, though, she had to explain to Mrs. Stoddard. One step at a time. One day at a time. There was no way around it. She'd faced too many challenges to be afraid of this one. If Mrs. Stoddard kicked her out, she would find a way to survive until Luke came for her. And if Luke didn't want her, she'd just go on . . . somehow. One thing was certain—she would love this baby to the depths of her soul.

The back door burst open then, and Sally came inside, her eyes red and puffy. Annie's heart pounded with dread. Luke? Jeremiah? "What's wrong, Sally?"

The girl sniffled and sat down at the table. "Jake."

Annie put a hand to her heart and closed her eyes. "He was on the list?"

"Yes," Sally answered, her voice sounding small and distant. She broke into harder tears, and Annie's head ached.

Their only remaining brother was dead. Somehow, she'd known all along that Jake, too, was gone from her life forever. She felt strangely calm. It was just her and Sally now . . . and the baby. The baby. "Sally."

Her sister's shoulders shook in sobs as she wiped at her eyes and faced Annie.

"We have to be strong," Annie told her. "I know all of this has been awful for you, too. But we have to thank God we still have each other. And we have to thank God for . . . for the fact that as one life is taken, another is created."

Sally frowned through tears. "What do you mean?"

Annie figured this was the best way to soothe her sister's heart and take her mind off her sorrow. "I'm going to have a baby, Sally, and I want you to know that it's Jeremiah's."

Sally's eyes widened, and she blinked. Annie could tell that the girl was trying to comprehend the news and make sense of it. "But . . . *Luke* is your husband."

"Yes, he is. And I love him, but before that, I loved Jeremiah. It just never worked out. And then when Jeremiah found and rescued us, risked his life for us . . . I don't know . . . something happened. I remembered how much I'd always loved him, too . . . and I was scared and lonely and not sure Luke would ever come back to me. Sometimes things happen between a man and a woman that just can't be explained. Someday you will understand. I just hope . . . I hope you can forgive me. This baby will be your niece or nephew, and I might find myself completely alone in raising it. I'll need your help."

Sally slowly nodded. "I'd never be mad at you for that, Annie. You're all I have left in the whole world. And I love Jeremiah, too, for what he did for us."

Annie thought what an innocent, forgiving person her sister was. "I still have to explain this to Mrs. Stoddard. I'm starting to show now and have no choice."

"I hope she won't be mad."

"I just don't want her to feel ashamed to have me here. Maybe if I offer not to show myself in public or to her guests, she'll allow us to stay. And I'm banking on her husband's friendship with Jeremiah."

Sally swallowed. "What about Luke?"

Annie sighed. "I'll face that matter when I get to it. First, he has to—"

"Annie! Annie!" Her name was shouted by Grace Stoddard, who came rushing into the kitchen, skirts rustling. The stout woman waved a letter. "I just picked this up in town! It's from Luke!"

Annie gasped, setting the silver polish and rag aside.

"Oh, Annie, open it! Open it!" Sally cried, rushing around to stand behind her.

Her hands shaking, Annie took the letter from Mrs. Stoddard and studied it for a moment, hardly able to believe it really was Luke's handwriting . . . his name on the envelope. Luke! He was alive!

"Let's leave your sister alone to read the letter," Mrs. Stoddard suggested to Sally.

"But I want—"

"I think she should be alone," Mrs. Stoddard repeated. "Annie can share it with you after she's had a chance to read it herself."

"Mrs. Stoddard, I have to tell you, our brother's name was on the roster today," Sally told her. "Jake is dead!"

"Oh, dear Lord, I'm so sorry." The woman put an arm around Sally and led her out of the room, consoling her as they walked.

Annie stared at the letter for several long seconds before finally opening it. She struggled against tears so she could see the writing.

My dearest Annie, it read. *I was wounded in a raid the first of February, but I am fine now. I am with Jeremiah.*

"Thank God!" she said aloud. They were together!

Jeremiah told me all about what happened to you at Fort Harmar, and I can't begin to tell you how sorry I am. I pray you will forgive me, Annie, for leaving you, yet that you will understand why I had to go. I have so much to tell you, but that will have to wait until I can hold you in my arms again. Just know that I think about you every minute of every day, but something happened that has compelled me to stay with this war until it is finished. Now that I know you are well and safe, I can continue the fight without worrying, thanks to Jeremiah, and to George Washington's good friends there in Philadelphia. Thank God for Jeremiah and his skill in finding you, and then finding me. Now he and I are together and can look out for each other. We are headed for New York to find George Washington and offer our services.

So, they would both continue fighting. And she would continue living the hell of not knowing if either of them would make it back to her.

I love you, Annie. You will never know how much. There is no explaining it. My regrets are many. I don't know what we will do when I return, but I promise you I will come for you before the year is out. If you still want me, we will build a new life together. In love and prayers, I am yours. Luke

Annie folded the letter, tears welling in her eyes. *If you still love me.* How could he think otherwise? "The question, Luke, is, will *you* still want *me*?" she muttered softly.

Thank God he was alive, and that he was with Jeremiah.

Would Jeremiah tell him what had happened between them in the cave? Even if he did, that shock would not be as great as coming home to find her carrying Jeremiah's child . . . for even Jeremiah didn't know.

37

"Damn, it's hot!" Luke wiped at sweat on his face with his shirt-sleeve.

"This sure isn't the kind of day I would pick for battle," Jeremiah answered. He removed his shirt.

"Jesus, Jeremiah, you'll be naked as an Indian."

"Yeah? Well, maybe Indians have better sense when it comes to hot weather. You and the others can swelter under those shirts if you want. I'm for taking mine off. Guess I've lived with the Indians too often."

Luke chuckled. "Hell, you're as dark as one, I'll say that."

Jeremiah slung his musket back around his shoulder. "You run a close second. That tan just makes your eyes look bluer. You should take your shirt off and get some sun on your back."

"I don't think General Greene would appreciate that. When we attack, we should be in uniform."

"Well, I've never been one to follow protocol, as you well know."

Luke leaned against a moss-covered tree. "I just wish Greene would hurry up and give the call to attack. The Redcoats down there are ripe for picking."

Moving through heavy forest near Eutaw Springs, the Continentals had spied a large contingent of English soldiers heading east along the road to Charleston. The soldiers had stopped to forage in a field of sweet potatoes.

Jeremiah moved to the edge of the bank and opened his telescope. "There must be over two thousand men down there," he said quietly.

Luke studied his brother's scarred back, the sight only cementing his resolve that staying in this war was the right thing to do. "Yeah? Well, we have even more men than that," he answered.

"And we have the advantage of surprise." Jeremiah closed the telescope and turned to face his brother. "Want to take a look?"

"No thanks." Luke closed his eyes. "I have a feeling I'll see my share of Redcoats in just a few minutes and I won't have time for counting."

Jeremiah's dark eyes literally glittered with eagerness. "This is it, brother. I have a feeling this war is just about over. With Cornwallis surrounded at Yorktown, and Washington and the French moving in on him there, this is pretty much England's last chance. I'll bet that if those soldiers down there get to Charleston, they'll be surrounded there, too. Before you know it, you'll be on your way home to Annie."

Luke slowly got to his feet, sweat running down his face. The humidity today was close to unbearable, and he longed for the cool, crisp Indian-summer weather of the Ohio Valley. He faced his brother. "We've been through a lot since coming back South from New York, haven't we?"

Jeremiah sobered. "That we have. And we've both had our fill of war and killing and guerrilla attacks."

"We should have always been together, Jeremiah. You should come back with me, help me rebuild the farm."

There was that odd sadness that he'd so often seen in his brother's eyes lately. Jeremiah shook his head. "That's for you and Annie to do, if you decide. I'd just be in the way." He slung his shirt around the back of his neck. "I'll head farther west, see what's out there in country that the white man has never seen yet. I'll bet there are Indian tribes out there we don't even know about."

"But we're just getting to know each other after too long apart. I'm finding we're more alike than I ever thought."

Jeremiah cast him a look that made Luke wonder what his brother was not telling him. "I agree with you there."

"So, why don't you make up your mind to settle down? You can't wander forever, Jeremiah."

"Yeah, well, I'll know when the time is right."

There was no more time for talking. Excited, whispered orders moved through the ranks to start heading down the hill, keeping to the trees. Jeremiah and Luke stayed together as they snuck quietly through brush and pine, ever closer to the unsuspecting English soldiers. They then crouched, each man taking aim at his chosen target. Finally came the command.

"Fire!"

Luke and Jeremiah each fired their first shot, as did the rest of the nearly twenty-four hundred men. Hundreds of Redcoat soldiers fell, and the Continentals yelled wildly as they surged forward for combat. Luke reloaded as he ran toward the enemy. He got off another shot, then lowered his musket to use the bayonet as he clashed with his first man.

The English soldiers were frantically trying to regroup, many of them fleeing the sweet-potato field with Continentals in pursuit. Luke rammed his bayonet into the gut of one man, whirled and shoved it into another soldier's side. The battle became one of stabbing, ducking, and chasing. He quickly lost track of Jeremiah as for the next hour, it was every man for himself.

Men fell everywhere. The Continentals pushed forward as the English on the front lines fought desperately to retain their turf. The fighting became a din of gunfire and screams of pain, clashing swords and bayonets, grunts and growls, and a confusion of orders. Sweat poured into Luke's eyes, making it difficult for him to see what he was doing.

He felt a blow from behind and he fell forward, then rolled onto his back to see Jeremiah ram his own bayonet into an English soldier who was about to stab Luke while he was down.

"Let's go! They're running for the creek!" Jeremiah told him.

Luke got to his feet again, rubbing at a painful bump on the back of his head. Now the chase began to turn into an obstacle course as he and Jeremiah and others had to make their way over and around wounded and dead bodies, both Continental and English. To Luke's amazement, he noticed a scalp hanging from Jeremiah's belt, and fresh blood was splattered all over his brother's naked torso. At the moment, Jeremiah appeared all Indian, and Luke guessed he could sometimes be as wild as one.

Both men stabbed and hit and shot and fought their way through the sweet-potato field toward the creek, the hunt-and-run battle dragging on in the awful heat. A new surge of English soldiers who'd managed to regroup came at them and yet more hand-to-hand combat ensued, the din of battle increasing again.

For nearly two more hours, Luke was too busy staying alive to know what was happening with Jeremiah or anyone else. Each side would surge toward the other for more battle, then withdraw and regroup. Over and over, Luke clashed with English soldiers to his right, his left, behind him, ahead of him, dodging, stabbing, running. Some of those who fought along with the English wore Tory uniforms, some wore normal clothing, obviously Loyalists who'd joined the English soldiers to help boost their numbers.

Finally, those English soldiers still not wounded or dead retreated to the opposite bank of Eutaw Creek. Greene ordered the Continentals to pull back and regroup, an order Luke thought was a mistake. They had the English on the run. Why give them time to regroup yet again and set up a counterattack? Watching them scurry around on the other side of the distant creek, Luke was reminded of a hive of bees gathering for attack, yet when he turned, to his dismay, he saw that many of the now nearly starved Continentals used the break in the battle to begin foraging in the potato field!

Luke was astounded. This was a perfect opportunity to continue pushing the English toward Charleston and perhaps take the town. Jeremiah caught up with him then, breathing heavily.

"You all right?"

"So far. You?"

"Same."

"Can you believe this? Why are we letting up?"

Jeremiah shook back his hair, which was wet with perspiration. "You've got me."

Luke glanced at the scalp on Jeremiah's belt. "My God, Jeremiah, we're supposed to be civilized men."

Jeremiah looked around. "Well, Luke, I don't see much that's civilized about this war. And don't forget, our great-grandmother was Mohawk."

Both men laughed, and the moment was suddenly so peaceful that when a hole suddenly opened in Jeremiah's chest, it took a few seconds for Luke to realize what had just happened. Jeremiah stared at him in dismay, an odd regret suddenly coming into his eyes. He crumpled to the ground.

Luke blinked in disbelief, then turned to see a wounded

English soldier on his knees, staring at both of them, a smoking pistol in his hand.

Luke felt the blood drain from his face. Shock and horror engulfed him. He tore over to the wounded Englishman and ran his bayonet into the man's chest, enjoying the look of terror on his face. He yanked out the bayonet, and hardly able to breathe, he turned back to Jeremiah, who lay on his back in the potato field, blood flowing from the middle of his chest. "No!" he screamed. "God, no!" He ran to Jeremiah, dropping his musket and kneeling beside his brother. "Jeremiah!"

Jeremiah looked at him with eyes glazed in a way Luke had seen all too often in this war . . . eyes that told him the life remaining in Jeremiah was ebbing away.

"Hang on, Jeremiah! Don't die on me! Not now!"

Jeremiah grasped hold of the front of Luke's shirt. "You . . . have . . . Annie."

Luke frowned, tears beginning to flow. "That's not the same! Don't die, Jeremiah! Come home with me to the valley! We'll rebuild! You and me and Annie, we'll—"

"Don't . . . ever . . ." His hand dropped away from its grip on Luke.

Luke leaned closer to hear his brother's weakened voice. "What is it, Jeremiah?" He shook with sobs, struggling to be still and hear his voice.

"Don't stop . . . loving her."

Luke straightened and ripped off his shirt, wadding it up and pressing it against Jeremiah's wound. "I don't know what you mean, Jeremiah. Why would I stop loving her?"

"Annie. You've got . . . Annie. Don't ever . . . let her go. I . . . loved her, too."

Luke shook his head. "Jeremiah—"

"She loves you ... more than you ... know. Tell her ... I love her."

"Jeremiah, hang on! You can tell her yourself!" Luke cared little at the moment just what Jeremiah was talking about. He only knew his brother was dying. Jeremiah was dying! How could this be? Men like Jeremiah didn't die. He was a strong, virile, fighting man. He could fight several men at once. He pressed harder on the shirt to try to stop the bleeding. "Come on, Jeremiah! Hang on!"

"... love you, Luke. Sorry I ... wasn't more help ... with the farm."

"Jeremiah, I—" Luke could see more life slipping away. "I love you, too, Jeremiah. Just hang on! You're strong in body and in will. You can ..."

The life left Jeremiah's eyes. Luke just stared at him, stunned. How could they be talking and laughing one moment and in the next, all the life be gone out of his brother? "Jeremiah," he groaned. "My God!" A wrenching sob engulfed him, and in the next breath, he screamed his brother's name. *"Jerrrri-iiimiiiiaaah!"*

Others now came running to see what happened, including Preacher Falls, who instantly fell to his knees and began praying. Luke bent over his brother and wept. Finally, the others pulled him away.

"Don't leave him here!" Luke screamed. "Take him up the hill so I can bury him. Don't leave him here to rot in the sun!"

Preacher Falls asked some of the men to help him carry Jeremiah's body off the field, and for the next hour or so, several men dug feverishly with hands and bayonets, a few using spades they'd retrieved from the remains of the English camp in the sweet-potato field. They finally dug deep enough to bury

Jeremiah, but his body had to be bent from the waist in order for it to fit into the hole.

Preacher Falls gave a eulogy and prayer, and just as they finished, the British came marching across the creek and began attacking the Continentals still in the potato field. Preacher Falls and the others were forced to leave the burial to go and fight again.

Luke, consumed with grief, began pushing dirt back into the hole where Jeremiah's doubled-up body lay, still shirtless. Right now, he did not regret killing one Tory or Loyalist or English soldier.

Amid tears, Luke finished filling the hole and pressed down on the dirt. He noticed a large rock nearby, and he walked over and pulled, rolled, and shoved it until the rock lay over the grave. Somehow, he had to mark this spot, where Jeremiah Wilde would lie forever. His name would now be added to the rosters of the dead.

38

Philadelphia

"Just try to breathe deeply and push, Annie." Grace Stoddard rushed about with towels and hot water, while Sally bent over Annie, trying to wash away her perspiration with a cool cloth.

"You'll be okay, Annie," the young girl assured her.

Annie rolled her eyes, thinking how little her sister knew about the pain she was experiencing. Now came another one, that deep, ripping, wrenching cramp that meant her body was trying to expel the baby in her belly. She could not help screaming.

"Just let it come, dear." The words were spoken by Edna Carlisle, a neighboring woman who'd given birth to six children and who'd helped many other women deliver their babies. "You're fighting it."

"The . . . pain," Annie groaned, drenched in sweat in spite of the day's chilly weather.

"I know, but it will be over soon, and believe me, it's a pain easily forgotten," Edna told her.

At the moment, Annie found that hard to believe. She lay

on her bed in the upstairs room where she'd kept to herself the last four months, choosing not to embarrass Mrs. Stoddard by walking around the house in her pregnant condition. Mrs. Stoddard had been kind and nonjudgmental, but Annie could tell that the woman was uneasy about the situation.

At last the baby was coming ... Jeremiah's baby. She'd lost Luke's child, and now she was having his brother's baby. It was all so unreal. In her last letter from Luke, he was heading south with Jeremiah, and both thought the war would end soon. What was she going to do if they came back to Philadelphia together? They finally were growing closer. She could tell by Luke's letters. This baby could destroy that closeness.

She could only pray that God would help her find a way to rectify this situation. For now, the fact remained that a baby would be born. Another labor pain tore through her, bringing another scream. She'd lain in labor for over twelve hours, and both Edna and Grace had warned her that the first babies were usually the hardest to deliver.

Still ... this was not really her first baby. She'd lost her first child to war. How strange that only a little over a year ago, she and Luke both thought this war could never affect their lives on the frontier. How wrong they had been. Now here she lay in Philadelphia, hundreds of miles from Willow Creek, giving birth to another man's baby.

Suddenly the labor became even more intense—deep, grinding pains—and Edna was telling her to "Push! Push!" Annie thought how silly it was to think she could control the pushing. Her body took over, and her muscles seemed to have a mind of their own.

"It's coming!" The women's voices became distant and excited. She heard her own screams, yet wondered where they came from. Through the two women's orders and exclamations and

Sally's encouraging support, she finally heard a smack, a little squeal, and someone shouted, "It's a boy!"

A boy! A son for Jeremiah! Annie heard Edna say something about afterbirth, and there came more pain as someone pushed and massaged her stomach.

"He's perfect!" someone said.

Of course he'd be perfect. Jeremiah was a strong, handsome, perfect man. Luke's baby would also have been perfect.

More rushing around . . . someone washed her . . . she sat up so someone could slip a clean gown on her . . . clean blankets were laid over her . . . and minutes later, a tiny little boy wrapped in his own blanket was laid beside her.

"Here's your new son," Edna told her.

"Oh, Annie, he's so tiny!" Sally exclaimed.

Annie turned her head and managed to raise up on one elbow to look down at her son. "Someday he'll be a big, tall, strong man," she said lovingly, her eyes tearing.

"What's his name?" Sally asked.

Annie opened the blanket partway and studied the baby's ruddy red skin and shock of dark hair. His little arms flailed and he kicked his legs upward, letting out a tiny wail.

"Jeremiah," she answered Sally. "He must be called Jeremiah."

39

Annie laid baby Jeremiah in his cradle. He'd fallen asleep feeding at her breast, and for a while, she'd simply watched him, studying his perfect little face, his long fingers, the way his little mouth pursed in his sleep. She pushed soft cotton into her bodice to help soak up excess milk, then buttoned her dress and draped a shawl over herself to hide any signs of leaking milk.

She turned then to gaze out the upstairs window at the changing leaves. Winter would come soon. Just a year ago, Fort Harmar had been attacked and she was carried off by the Shawnee, spending part of last winter as their captive. She had so much to thank Jeremiah for: for saving her . . . for finding and staying with Luke . . . for her beautiful son . . . for so much.

She prayed that the war would not last another whole winter, that it would not be another full season before she saw either Jeremiah or Luke again, that God would keep them both safe.

The street below was wet from a chilly rain, and she watched a coach splash through a puddle and pull up in front of the house. A man exited and looked up, as though trying to determine if he was in the right place. He wore dark pants and high black boots, a rather plain dark-woolen jacket—simple clothing similar to what was given to men by the new government after leaving service in—

"Luke!" she whispered. "My God, it's Luke!" She shouted the words the second time. She turned and ran to the bedroom door, running out into the upstairs hallway and down the curved stairway at the end of the hall. She hesitated on the first landing when there was a knock at the door, then hurried a little farther down the stairs, freezing in place when Grace Stoddard answered the door. She heard Luke ask if Annie Wilde was still living there.

"You must be Luke!" Grace exclaimed. "You look just like your brother, except for those blue eyes!" She stepped back. "Come in! Come in!"

Luke stepped inside.

"Annie's upstairs. I'll go—" Before Grace finished her sentence, Luke had already spied Annie standing on the stairway. For a moment, they just looked at each other . . . so much to say . . . so much time to make up for . . . so many explanations necessary between them . . . so much for both of them to be sorry for.

"Luke!" Annie finally spoke, trying to hide the welling tears.

He walked closer. "You look . . . even more beautiful than I remembered." Another step up to the landing. "Annie, you can see!"

She nodded, looking him over. So tired. He looked so tired. And thinner, but still oh, so handsome, his eyes seeming even bluer against his tanned face. But there was something there— something terrible. Her stomach cramped with dread.

"I've so much to tell you, Annie. I'm so sorry . . . sorry I left you like that. Jeremiah told me what happened after I left. My God, Annie!"

"It wasn't your fault. You thought I was safe. None of us knows what will happen in life, Luke. I, too, have things to be sorry for."

He shook his head. "I can't imagine what you could possibly need to feel sorry for. And right now, it doesn't matter."

It matters more than you could know, she wanted to tell him. But for the moment, he looked ready to pass out. She descended what stairs were left, and in the next moment, she was in his arms. "Oh, Luke!"

He held her tight and turned to go down the rest of the stairs so he could hold her on the level floor.

"I'll leave you two alone," Grace said, walking out of the room.

Luke hugged Annie so tightly she thought she might not be able to get her breath. She could say nothing more than to speak his name, over and over.

"He's dead, Annie!" he groaned. "Jeremiah's dead!" He broke into sobbing, and as the words sank in, Annie thought she might faint.

Jeremiah! No, not Jeremiah! Men like him didn't die! How little Luke knew of her true devastation. She wept . . . hard, ripping sobs for losing the first love of her life . . . her baby's father . . . her husband's brother . . . the man who'd risked his life to rescue her . . . the man who'd taken away the ugliness of her rape. *God, no! Not Jeremiah!*

"Oh, Luke, I'm so sorry! And I thank God you're still here . . . and alive!" she sobbed. "I could have lost . . . both of you!"

After several minutes of tears, they managed to pull apart, and it tore at Annie's insides to see a man like Luke cry. She took a handkerchief from a pocket on her dress and wiped at her own tears, then reached up and gently wiped the tears from Luke's face. "My darling Luke, I'm so sorry."

He sniffled and ran a hand through his hair, sitting down on the stairs. "It was so crazy," he told her. He took a deep breath for self-control. "We'd been through so much, so many battles, hand-to-hand combat with knives and bayonets." He shook his head. "We'd just been through a tough fight by a creek in South Carolina, just west of Charleston." He put his head in his hands. "There we were, standing in a goddamn sweet-potato field, joking around. I mean, we weren't even engaged in fighting at the time. That's what's so damned ironic about it. We were talking one minute, and the next minute, a hole opened up in his chest and he just . . . stood there . . . like he wasn't even sure himself of what had just happened. A goddamn wounded Redcoat lying nearby sat up and just . . . shot him! Just like that! I couldn't believe what I was seeing!"

Jeremiah! If only she could have been there to tell him he had a son . . . to tell him good-bye! Annie sat down beside Luke, folding her arms around her aching stomach, wanting to scream Jeremiah's name. It didn't seem possible that she truly would never see him again. "I'm so sorry, Luke. So sorry for all you've been through."

"There is a lot more to tell you—things I've seen and done." He sniffled again and took another deep breath. "This has been a hard-won freedom, Annie, but after what happened at Willow Creek—and after some of the things I've seen, and what Jeremiah suffered while imprisoned on that ship—it's worth the fight. When this war is over, we'll start over, too. Somehow, we'll start over—if not at Willow Creek, then somewhere else. I'm thinking about . . . maybe we could find some free land farther north in Ohio, maybe up by Lake Erie. Jeremiah . . . he talked a lot about the Great Lakes, the opportunities farther west. Who knows what's out there? We might be able to start up some kind of trading business all over the Great Lakes—some kind of shipping business. I don't know. I've just . . . been thinking about all the possibilities." He wiped at his eyes and turned to her. "Right now, I just want to spend time with you and get our marriage back together. I love you so much, Annie . . . and I'm so glad you can see again."

She took his hand. "And I love you, Luke. Please know that I've always loved you, that the things that happened while you were gone . . . they were the result of terror . . ." She looked away. "Terror over being held captive, terror that I'd never see you again, terror that you could never look at me in the same way after the rapes, and after losing our baby. I felt so alone . . . so alone."

"Annie, my God, why would I blame you for any of those things?" He moved an arm around her. "What is it, Annie?"

How could she tell him? For several more minutes, they just sat there, crying in each other's arms. So much loss! How was anyone to bear so much loss? Jeremiah! Each mourned him for different reasons.

Finally, Annie drew on her remaining courage and she stood up. "Come upstairs, Luke. I have something to show you."

40

Fear of rejection and rebuke engulfed Annie as she headed up the stairs. It was time Luke knew. There was no waiting, and with Jeremiah gone . . . She stood at the bedroom door, looking up at Luke as he came closer. "I have to ask you something."

He nodded, frowning. "What is it, Annie?"

"If you had . . . been killed in battle and Jeremiah had lived . . . would you have been glad to know that your brother would have taken care of me for the rest of his life? That he might even . . . love me? Marry me?"

He looked confused. "I'd like nothing better, but—" He looked her over. "Annie, before Jeremiah died, he told me he . . . loved you, too. He said to tell you that."

Oh, how it hurt to imagine Jeremiah lying in a potato field, bleeding to death and speaking about her in his last words! More tears spilled down her cheeks, and when she wiped them away and met Luke's gaze again, she could see that Luke realized what Jeremiah really meant by his words.

"He also told me to never stop loving you," Luke added.

"And he told you about rescuing me and Sally from the Shawnee?"

"Of course."

Annie took a deep breath for courage. "Luke . . . your brother . . . isn't really dead. He still lives, through his son." She opened the bedroom door and nodded toward the wooden cradle that sat near the bed. "He's not quite a month old yet." She gripped the doorknob tightly and looked away as her husband just stood there at first, grasping the reality of her news. "He's mine, Luke. Mine and yours, if you have enough understanding and think you can love him, raise him as your own son, just as Jeremiah would want you to do. I gave him Jeremiah's name. He would have done the same for you if the tables were turned."

Slowly, Luke walked past her toward the cradle. He leaned over and pulled aside the coverlet, studying the sleeping baby for several long minutes.

"God has His reasons, Luke, for giving life. I loved Jeremiah when I was very young. You already know that. Then he left, and I thought he'd never come back. Actually, I loved both of you. I agreed to marry you because, like Jeremiah often said, you were the better man in so many ways. I loved you both for different reasons, but if not for that attack, for the things those men did to me, the terror of losing my sight, and then my mother being hacked to death right next to me, and then being taken captive by the Shawnee—" She swallowed back more tears. "How can I possibly explain it? Never, never would I have betrayed your love with any other man . . . and not even with Jeremiah under any other circumstances. He rescued me . . . and we were forced to hide in a tiny cave along the Mad River. I was terrified, more for Jeremiah than for myself, because I knew what the Shawnee would do to him if we were found. I still could barely see, and Jeremiah was right there the whole time . . . holding me . . . protecting me. And he loved me, too, Luke. He always did, but he knew he could never be a fit husband. You were the man I chose, the man I meant to honor and cherish the rest of my life. I still feel that way."

Luke kept studying the baby the whole time Annie spoke.

"Who knows why we do the things we do in times of war and raping and killing?" she continued. "I can only tell you that I truly believe God meant for this to happen . . . so that a little part of Jeremiah can live on and always be with us. And just as you would have wanted Jeremiah to take care of me, he would want you to be a father to his son. If you can never forgive me, I will understand. Just please don't take it out on that tiny little baby who carries your blood. He could just as well be yours as Jeremiah's."

Finally, he turned to face her. How she wished she could read his eyes! For several long seconds, he said nothing. The baby started fussing a little, making tiny squeaking sounds, his arms and legs beginning to flail. Luke looked at him again, put a hand into the cradle, letting the baby grasp a finger. Luke wiggled the finger and pulled a little. "Quite a grip," he said.

"Naturally," Annie answered. "He's Jeremiah's son."

Luke stared at the baby a moment longer before pulling his finger away. He turned to face her. "My father died fighting for one kind of freedom, and now Jeremiah has died fighting for another. My whole family is dead, Annie, and other than Sally, so is yours. That leaves you and me . . . and Jeremiah's son. You could never understand what this war is like, and I can never understand some of the things you suffered, what it would do to you. This is all that's left now. You. Me. Sally. And little Jeremiah. God knows we're lucky to have that much." He looked at the baby again. "After what you went through, I guess I can't blame you for what happened any more than you can blame me for running my bayonet through a boy barely ten years old."

Annie gasped, putting a hand to her chest, feeling his pain. "Oh, Luke!"

The child fussed more, and Luke removed his coat, reaching down to pick up the infant. He walked to the bed and sat down, cradling the baby against his chest. He kissed the child's head and closed his eyes. "It's all right, Jeremiah," he said softly. "Your daddy would have loved you far more than his own life. I'll do the same."

Annie's heart went out to him. Still, she wasn't sure how he truly felt until he looked up at her, surprising her with the look of love in his eyes. "Come sit down beside me, Annie."

Feeling weak in the legs, Annie walked over to the bed and sat down. Luke kissed the baby again, then stood up and returned little Jeremiah to the cradle. The child's eyes closed again. Luke turned to Annie and sat down on the bed again. He scooted back, then moved an arm around her waist and urged her to do the same, gently laying her close to him.

"You know what I want to do?" he asked.

"No."

He smiled sadly. "I want to sleep. Just sleep, and sleep, and sleep. And when I wake up, I want to see you lying beside me. And when we're both rested enough, I want to go home and just get on with our lives together, figure out what we're going to do and how we're going to do it . . . and I want to enjoy my new family, including my new son. Jeremiah would want that, don't you think?"

Annie managed a smile in spite of the pain that kept surging through her at the thought of Jeremiah being dead. "Yes, he'd want that. He always wanted that for you and me, Luke. He loved both of us."

Luke leaned over, kissing her gently, then hungrily—her

mouth, her eyes, her hair, her neck. "I love you so, Annie," he said. "But right now, I'm so goddamn tired."

"Of course you are." She sat up and pulled off his boots, then folded back the bed covers. "Go to sleep, Luke. And when you wake up, I'll be right here, just like you said you wanted. I won't leave this room until you wake up."

Luke crawled under the covers without undressing. He settled into bed, and Annie moved in beside him and stroked his thick dark hair away from his face.

"I still have money, Annie, in the stone house. It was hidden in a special place in the outside wall, behind a loose rock. Those outside walls still stand, and I doubt the Tories found the money. I'm going to go back and get it."

Annie kissed his cheek. "Jeremiah and I will go with you. And since those stone walls are still standing, we can rebuild, Luke. New crops can be planted."

"I used to dream about you sitting on the porch rocking our babies. Remember when I told you that?"

"I remember. And we *will* have more babies, yours and mine."

He smiled sadly and closed his eyes. In what seemed mere seconds, he was asleep.

Annie crawled off the bed and undressed, putting on her nightgown. She picked up a fussing Jeremiah and changed him, then fed him a little more until he, too, fell asleep again. She pulled him from her breast and laid him in his cradle, then crawled back into bed. She settled against Luke and fell asleep in his arms . . . in his strong, sure, loving arms. Never had she known such peace.

Just as he'd asked, when he awoke, she'd be right here beside him.

About the Author

Author/speaker Rosanne Bittner has penned over fifty American historical novels and has won numerous writing awards. She is a member of Women Writing the West, Romance Writers of America, Western Writers of America, the Oregon-California Trails Association, and the Montana, Michigan, and Nebraska Historical Societies. Ms. Bittner lives in a small town in southwest Michigan. She often travels for research and to conduct writing workshops.